Believe
a novella

Christmas in Mason

From *USA Today* Bestselling Author

Kelly Elliott

Visit my website at http://www.authorkellyelliott.com

ISBN-13: 978-0-9913096-3-4

Contents

1 Amanda

I stood at the sink, staring down at my hand that held the pregnancy test. I slowly smiled and felt my stomach do a few flip-flops.

Pregnant. I'm pregnant. I quickly wiped away the tear I felt rolling down my cheek as I closed my eyes and pictured Brad's face when I told him. I knew I wasn't very far along because I had just missed my period.

"Well?" Heather said on the other side of the door. "What does it say, Manda?"

I took a deep breath, turned and opened the door. When I opened it, there they were, Heather, Ellie and Ari, all standing with goofy-ass grins on their faces. I tried not to show it, but as soon as Ellie flashed me that smile of hers, I lost it and started crying.

"Oh no…oh God, please tell me those are happy tears!" Heather said as she pulled me into her arms.

I was so happy I couldn't even talk. I pulled back and nodded my head and the three of them started screaming.

I started laughing as I watched them all jump up and down. "Congratulations sweets!" Ari said as she gave me a hug and whispered in my ear. "Brad's gonna be over the moon."

I smiled at her as she pulled away and winked at me. I had shared with Ari how much Brad had wanted another baby. He wanted so badly to be a part of our next pregnancy. I knew it was because of the guilt he lived with by missing so much of my pregnancy with Maegan. We had been trying for the last five months, and it was starting to take a toll on Brad.

"I guess that trip a few weeks back helped," I said as I winked at her.

Ari and Jeff had arranged a cruise for Brad and I, and it took everything I had to leave Maegan with her.

"Hell yeah it did! I told you all you had to do was just relax," Ari said.

As we all made our way onto Heather's back porch deck, Ellie and Heather were going a mile a minute, talking about the two new additions to our little group. Ellie was due in May, and if my math in my head was right, I would be due mid to late August.

"Are you going to find out if it's a boy or a girl?" Heather asked as she sat down and put her feet up. She looked so damn beautiful, and I … I'd never seen her so happy.

I shrugged my shoulders. I felt funny even talking about it, with Brad not knowing yet and with me only being about three weeks pregnant.

Ellie looked at me and tilted her head. "You want to tell Brad, don't you? Before you talk too much about it, huh?"

Jesus, how does this girl do that? "Christ, Ells, you getting the gift of knowing all?" I said with a giggle.

Everyone let out a small laugh and Ellie rolled her eyes. "I just know if it was me, I wouldn't want to really talk about it until I told Gunner."

Ari nodded her head. "Shit, when I went with her to the doctor and she found out she was pregnant I wasn't allowed to say a word about it until she told Gunner."

Ellie shrugged her shoulders and took a sip of her tea. I laughed as I placed my hand on my stomach.

Heather looked and me and said, "How is Brad doing, Manda? Have you heard from his parents?"

I shook my head and just the mention of his parents made my blood boil. "Nope, not a word. His mom tried to threaten us with legal action because they wanted to see Maegan, but Brad went to their house one night for dinner and that was the end of it. He came home and told me we wouldn't have to worry about them doing it again. He seemed so sad, and when I asked him what had happened, he told me not to worry or ever think about his parents threatening us again."

I looked down and away and felt the tears building in my eyes. I felt Ari put her hand on my leg. I looked at each of them and saw the love in their eyes.

I swallowed and cleared my throat. "I know it's better this way, but I can't help but feel like it's my fault that Brad walked away from his own parents. His future was set, ya know? I mean he would have taken over his father's business, had more money than we would have known what to do with it and...and Maegan would know both sets of her grandparents."

"Manda, you can't keep doing this," Ellie said.

"I know. Believe me I know them being out of our lives has been the best thing for all three of us, but it still makes me sad. It's his parents. I mean his dad was always okay, just his mother."

Ari shook her head and said, "If they really cared, they would have never have done the things that they did, Amanda. I mean I know most of it was the evil bitch who shall not be named, but still, Brad's father stood by and allowed her evil to take place."

I let out a giggle and nodded in agreement.

"I know this. Really I do. I'm just glad I have such a close relationship with my own parents and that at least Maegan will have two grandparents that love her more than life itself."

I sat back in my chair and thought about last night and how Brad had made such slow sweet love to me.

"Holy hell, Manda, what in the hell are you thinking about? Your face is red as your shirt!" Heather said.

I threw my hands up to my cheeks and busted out laughing. "Oh God…I was thinking about being with Brad last night."

All three of them leaned forward with wide-ass grins on their face.

"Oh yeah? Tell us. I've always thought that boy was probably a good screw."

Ellie, Heather and I all shouted, "Ari!"

"What? Don't tell me the first time you saw that tall, dark-haired handsome man you didn't think he would be good in bed!" Ari said as she looked at Ellie, and then Heather, and then looked at me and raised one eyebrow.

I shook my head and said, "Yes. Yes I did think that, but my God. What if I asked you if Jeff was good in bed? No wait!" I put my hands up and started shaking them. "Forget I even said that."

Ellie and Heather started laughing.

Ari leaned back and smiled as she took a sip of tea and then said, "Hey, ask me anything you want. I have no problem bragging about how good of a fu—"

"Stop!" Ellie shouted. "Please just stop, Ari. I don't need, nor do I want, to know what my brother is like in the sex department with you."

I smiled as I shook my head. "No really though, Brad is doing so good. I'm so proud of how he is handling things now. I've asked him if he ever has the desire to take anything and he told me no. Just one look at Maegan and me and he knows what he would lose. I'm so happy y'all. I mean, it's never been better." I let my head drop back as I could almost feel his lips on my skin. "I mean…*fuck*…how does it keep getting better? Wouldn't you think after a few years of marriage and a baby things would seem…normal?"

Heather let out a giggle. "Nope. I feel the same way. Like every time gets better. No matter if it's a quickie or a long romantic evening."

Ari and Ellie both nodded their heads. "I agree. I swear every morning when I wake up and look at Gunner, I fall in love with him more."

"Same here. What about when they touch you? Like Jeff will grab my hand and I still get those butterflies in my stomach."

"Yes!" We all yelled out with a giggle.

"What's your favorite thing they do to you while they're making love to you?" I asked as I looked at each of my best friends.

"Oh…damn, that's hard 'cause Jeff does…"

"Let's hear from Heather first, shall we? I need to work my stomach up to whatever in the hell it is you're going to say about my brother," Ellie said as she made a funny face.

"Fine. Heather, you first," said Ari as she rolled her eyes at Ellie.

"Oh wow…I like when he holds my hands above my head and looks deep into my eyes as he tells me how much he loves me."

"That's it?" Ari asked, sounding disappointed.

Heather's mouth dropped open and she "What do you mean, 'that's it'? What were you expecting?"

Ari gave Heather a wicked smile and said, "I don't know. Some bondage thrown in there I guess."

Heather reached down and picked up a toy and threw it at Ari. "Fuck you, Ari!"

Ari started laughing as Ellie and I tried to hold in our laughter.

"Okay, okay…my turn," Ellie said with a huge smile. "I absolutely love it when Gunner kisses on my neck and then slowly moves his way up to my ear and barely whispers to me that he's about to come. Oh God…it sends me over the edge every time."

"Hell yeah…the quiet-don't-wake-the-kids lovemaking. So romantic and hot," Ari said as she wiggled her eyebrows up and down. Ellie smiled and nodded her head.

Ari looked at me and said, "Your turn."

I smiled and tried to pick one of the things that I loved. "Wow…this is harder than I thought. There are so many things that I love."

"I know, right?" Heather said.

"Um…okay I know. Mine is kind of after we've made love. Brad does it every single time, no matter if we just had a romantic lovemaking session or a hot-and-heavy fuck session."

"Fuck session?" Ari said with a laugh.

I rolled my eyes, "You know what I mean. Anyway, afterwards he always puts his hands on my face, kisses my nose and then looks into my eyes and says…"

They all leaned closer in with smiles spread across their faces.

"What does he say?" Heather asked, her voice almost a whisper.

I smiled and said, "He says, 'You're the most beautiful woman I've ever laid eyes on, Manda. I love making love to you more than anything. I love you so much, baby,' then he leans his forehead to mine and says, 'Thank you for loving me.'"

Heather, Ellie, and Ari all put their hands up to their chest and fell back in their chairs.

"Every time? He says the same thing every time?" Ellie asked.

I nodded my head and smiled. "Yep."

"Wow. That is so sweet," Ari said.

Heather pointed to Ari and said, "Your turn!"

Ari glanced over toward Ellie and said, "You ready?"

Ellie rolled her eyes and said, "Ugh…I guess so."

Ari took a deep breath and closed her eyes. She let a small smile play across her face and I couldn't help but giggle at the face Ellie was making.

"Holy hell…are you going to tell us or sit there and dream about it, for fuck's sake?" Ellie said as she folded her arms and looked at Ari.

Ari opened one eye and looked at Ellie. "Sorry, I was just imagining your brother making sweet passionate love to me."

"Gag me," Ellie said as she turned her head away from Ari.

Ari started laughing. "Okay, okay…so while Jeff and I are doing the nasty…"

"Stop!" Ellie said in a whiney voice.

Ellie reached over and slapped Ari on the arm.

After Ari stopped laughing, she looked down and said, "No really…I think one of my favorite things Jeff does while we are making love is how he talks to me. I mean, he really talks to me. Ya know? He either tells me how beautiful I am, or how much he loves me. He tells me how happy I make him. All the while he covers me in soft sweet kisses. God…just thinking about it gives me chills."

I glanced over towards Ellie and she was smiling. Just then I heard the guys. They had all walked down to the park with the kids. I loved seeing Josh pushing a stroller with two sleeping babies in it.

"Does Josh handle the twins good, Heather?" I asked as I peeked over at her watching him. The love pouring out from her eyes was hard to miss.

She looked at me and nodded her head. "He's amazing with them both, and he's not afraid to be alone with them. I love that."

Ari jumped up and walked towards Jeff. Luke was on his shoulders jabbering away.

Luke yelled out and Jeff stopped to take him off his shoulders. Ari bent down as Luke ran into her arms.

I looked at Gunner, who was carrying Alex on his shoulders as well. Ellie got up and walked over to them. I laughed when Alex started crying as Gunner tried to take her down.

"Daddy's girl," Ellie said as Alex smiled down at her.

Brad looked up at me and I had to catch my breath. He smiled at me, and I … if I had been standing, I would have had to grab onto something to hold myself up. He winked at me and started laughing. I slowly got up and made my way down to him.

I walked up to him and stood on my tippy toes to give him a kiss. He put his hand behind my neck and held me against his lips as he deepened the kiss. It took everything I had not to let out a moan. He pulled back and whispered, "I missed you, pumpkin."

"I missed you too." I looked at Maegan, who was smiling. I stepped back and held out my arms and she smiled bigger as I took her into my arms. I gave her a good smell and Brad laughed as he kissed Maegan on the top of the head. I couldn't help it; I had to smell her each time. I loved how she smelled.

We all made our way back to the deck. Ari put Luke down to play with Alex in the grass. Before I could even ask, Heather said, "There are no ants, Manda, so don't worry."

I giggled and set Maegan down next to Alex. I stood there and looked around as I took in the sight. Gunner was now sitting behind Alex, and Josh was talking to Brad and Jeff. Ellie went in to help Ari and Heather with the little ones. I put my hand on my stomach and tried to hold my smile in.

As I sat down and watched Gunner, Jeff, and Brad play with Maegan, Luke and Alex, I felt someone come up behind me. I felt Grace pulling my hair and I started laughing. I turned around and saw her beautiful smile looking right at me as Ari held her.

"My God, Ari she is going to break hearts," I said as Ari moved around me, sat down and held Grace up in front of her. She smiled.

"I know she is." Then she looked at me and asked, "When are you going to tell him?"

I bit down on my lower lip. "Two days."

"Christmas Eve. Can you wait two days?"

I let out a chuckle. "Hell, I don't know. I'm dying to tell him but I want to make it special for him." I peeked over at her and she gave me a weak smile.

"I understand, but Manda, no matter how you tell him, he is going to be beyond excited. You know that, right?"

I nodded my head as I looked back at the man I loved more than anything. To think we almost didn't make it to where we were today.

I closed my eyes and silently thanked God. When I opened them again Brad was looking at me. The look in his eyes caused me to suck in a breath of air. It was like he was looking deep into my soul.

I never took my eyes off of him but asked Ari, "Do you think Brad knows?"

I pulled my eyes from his and quickly looked at Ari, who was now looking at Brad. She looked back at me and said, "I think that boy is just head over heels in love with you, Amanda."

I looked back at him and he was still watching me. I slowly licked my lips and then put my index finger in my mouth and barely bit down on it. I could see the look in his eyes change. He stood up and walked over to Josh and said something to him. Josh jumped up and so did Gunner. They each held their hands out for Brad to shake them.

Ellie came walking out of the house and I jumped up quickly.

"Jesus H. Christ, Amanda, you just scared the hell out of me," Ari said. Grace started laughing at Ari jumping.

"Ells, I'm still bringing the desserts and ham for Christmas, right?" I asked as I reached down and kissed Grace and then Ari on the cheek.

Ellie nodded her head and said, "Yeah but are y'all leaving? Already?"

Ari threw her head back and said, "Ells…the hormones must have kicked in. Look at her…she has that look in her eyes."

I just looked at Ari and gave her a dirty look. Heather came walking out and smiled at everyone as she said, "The twins are sleeping!" I couldn't help but chuckle at how happy and relieved she sounded.

"Sweets, we are taking off. I'll see you Christmas Eve," I said as I walked up and gave Heather a kiss and hug good-bye.

As we walked to the car, Brad grabbed my hand. *Yep, there went the butterflies.*

I looked up at him and winked. The smile that spread across his face made my knees feel weak. *God, I want him so damn much.*

Brad was putting Maegan in her car seat as he looked at me and said, "We seriously have to think about buying a house closer to our friends."

I tilted my head and smiled. "Really? 'Cause I would love that, but you can't drive that far. What made you say that?"

"Well, for one thing, I love spending time with everyone, and the second thing is if we lived closer, I could get you home faster so I could make love to you longer."

I bit down on my lower lip. "Oh."

He let out a sexy-ass laugh and said, "Come on pumpkin, let's get home so I can give you some much needed attention."

I felt my face blush as I looked away and then back at him.

Oh Lord. Trying to not tell him about the baby was going to be very hard.

Very hard indeed.

2 Brad

After we got Maegan settled and in bed, Amanda and I both crashed onto the sofa. I looked over at her yawning and I couldn't help but smile. She looked beautiful. There was something about her tonight that just made her…glow. Her face was glowing and she just seemed so happy.

"Manda, are you happy?" I asked her as she snapped her head over to look at me.

She slowly smiled and I couldn't help but smile back at her. "I've never been so happy in my entire life. Are you happy?"

I reached over and pulled her onto my lap as I pushed her hair back and placed my hand on her face. "I'm so happy that sometimes I feel like I have to pinch myself because I think this is all just a dream. You, me and Maegan." I felt a pain in my chest for just a brief moment. We had been trying to get pregnant for the last five months and I was starting to think it just wasn't meant to be.

Amanda used her index finger to pull my face towards her. "It's going to happen." I smiled and shook my head. *How did she know I was thinking about a baby?*

I sucked in a deep breath and quickly let it out as I looked into her eyes. Her green eyes were the most beautiful green I'd ever seen. "I love you, Amanda." I whispered.

"I love you too."

I tilted my head and smiled at her. "You want to go and try and make a baby?" Her smiled dropped and she sucked in a breath of air. I knew she was getting stressed about not getting pregnant. I just want to believe that I didn't do any harm to myself with the drug use or that this was in some way a form of punishment.

She gave me a sexy grin and climbed off my lap. I sat there and watched as she pulled her t-shirt up and over her head.

Damn, this girl is perfect in every way. She moved her hands down and started to unbutton her jeans. She smiled as she slowly slid them down, exposing the white lace thong panties she had on. I moved my eyes up and down her body. Her light red hair was just below her shoulders and looked beautiful against her skin.

I licked my lips as she moved her hands up her body and unclasped her bra. My heart was beating a mile and minute, and I swore it was like I was going to see her naked for the first time. Her bra dropped and I bit down on my lower lip as she threw her head back and began touching her breasts.

Holy fucking shit. "Manda," was all I could get out as she snapped her head back up and slowly moved her hands down to her panties and slipped her hand inside them. *Is she trying to kill me? She's never done anything like this before.*

I swallowed hard and tried to move as I watched her feel on herself with one hand and play with her nipples with her other hand. I thought I was going to pass out from all the blood rushing to my dick.

I stood up and grabbed her neck and pulled her to me as I began to kiss her. The sounds she was making were driving me crazy. She pulled her hand out of her panties and began pulling at my hair.

"Manda, are you trying to kill me?" I whispered against her lips.

"Brad…I'm so horny and I want you so badly."

I reached down and picked her up as I carried her upstairs to our bedroom. The whole time we never stopped kissing.

Please don't let this be a dream…

I placed her gently down on the bed and she looked at me. "Touch yourself again," I said. She smiled and pulled her panties completely off and dropped them to the side of the bed. She put her hands on her body and slid them down; stopping at her stomach, she closed her eyes before moving her hand further down.

I quickly took my shirt and pants off and removed my boxers as I watched her touch on herself. *Hottest fucking thing I've ever seen.*

"Brad…" she whispered. She looked like she was getting close to coming so I crawled onto the bed and buried my face between her legs.

"God yes!" she cried out. I slipped my fingers inside of her and moaned at how wet she was. Before I knew it she was calling out my name. I looked up at her as she grabbed onto the sheets and arched her back as she came. There was nothing I loved more than making her feel good. I reached my hand up and placed it on her stomach and she bucked and then I saw the tears. I instantly stopped and sat up.

"Pumpkin? What's wrong? Why are you crying?" I asked. She quickly wiped the tears away.

She smiled big and said, "I'm just so happy, Brad. You make me feel so loved and I just…I guess I'm just really happy."

I quickly ran into the bathroom and rinsed out my mouth, I just wanted to kiss her and I knew how she was…no way she would let me after I just gave her oral sex.

I walked back in and she was laying there…smiling as she held her hand out to me. I walked over and took her hand and kissed it as I moved on top of her.

"Love me, Brad. Please love me," she whispered against my neck. I slowly moved to where I was teasing her with my tip before I buried myself deep inside her.

"God Amanda, you feel so good."

"I love you, Brad. I love you so much." She whispered as I made sweet love to her. I didn't want it to end so every time I felt like I was about to come I would stop and begin kissing her. "Please tell me I'm not dreaming," I said as I kissed down her neck.

"You're not…dreaming…Brad…please go faster," she begged as I stopped moving.

As I began moving again she arched herself and pulled me closer to her. It didn't take long before her orgasm caused me to let go. I softly called her name over and over as I poured myself into her. Pleading with God to please let her get pregnant.

I kept my weight off of her as I covered her face and neck with kisses. Once I got my breath back, I placed my hands on her face and looked into her eyes. I always wanted her to know how I felt about her. I never wanted her to ever doubt my love for her.

"You're the most beautiful woman I've ever laid eyes on, Manda. I love making love to you more than anything. I love you so much, pumpkin." I gently kissed her nose and winked at her.

I watched as her eyes filled with tears. I rolled over and brought her with me as we lay on our sides and just looked into each other's eyes. I wiped away the tear that was slowly making a trail down her cheek towards her ear.

"Baby, why are you crying again?"

She let out a small giggle and put her hand on the side of her face. "Do you know you say that to me every single time we finish making love? I love it so much and I can't even begin to tell you how special it makes me feel."

It felt like my chest exploded. I smiled and said, "Good. I want you know how special you are to me and how much I love you. I'd be lost without you." I closed my eyes and opened them again. "I just thank God every day you didn't walk away from me."

She shook her head and said, "Never. I'll love you until the day I die."

I leaned closer to her and kissed her. "I guess we should get some sleep. I still have a few more presents to buy Meg and we need to bring everything out to Gunner and Ells the next morning."

She laughed and sat up. "Brad! You are going to spoil this child. She has so many toys now."

"I know, but it's her first Christmas, Manda. It has to be special," I said. I looked at her with pleading eyes.

She laughed and flopped back down on the bed. "She's not even going to remember this Christmas."

I pulled her closer to me and said, "But we will."

"Okay…I'll give you that. Fine. But only for a couple of hours. I have stuff to do tomorrow before we head to Mason."

I smiled knowing she wanted to go and buy more toys just as much as I did. "It's a deal. Let's keep some presents home for when your parents come over Christmas evening."

She nodded her head and mumbled something before I heard her breathing slow down and my angel was fast asleep.

I closed my eyes and tried to get some sleep but every time I fell asleep I kept waking up to the same dream. Amanda standing in a field smiling at me and as I moved closer to her I saw her pregnant stomach. Right before I would get to her, I would wake up. *Every single time.*

I sat up in bed and looked at the clock. It was almost six in the morning. Maegan would be waking up soon. I looked at Amanda, who was sleeping like a baby. I quietly crawled out of bed and threw on my boxers as I made my way downstairs. I went to the kitchen and looked in the refrigerator. I pulled out the eggs, bacon and ham. I started to scramble the eggs as I put the bacon in another pan and reached under the cabinet for a frying pan for the ham.

I pulled out two glasses and put them on the table. I grabbed Meg's sippy cup and placed it next to the other cups. Then I took out the plates and put one down for each of us. As I turned to go back to the stove, I saw Amanda standing against the bar smiling.

"Whatcha doing?" she asked.

I smiled back and said, "I'm making my wife and daughter breakfast."

She pushed off the island and started walking towards me. "Maegan is still fast asleep." I noticed she had on a robe, which was weird, because Amanda was one to always get dressed when she woke up.

"Ahh…yeah she is, but…I um…" I looked down at her as she bit down on her lower lip. *Fuck…why was I getting so damn turned on?* I watched as she walked right up to the stove and turned everything off.

"Baby, I'm cooking and the eggs are…" I stopped immediately as I watched her open her robe and drop it to the floor.

"Holy shit," I said as I moved my eyes up and down her body. She was dressed in nothing but white lace panties. When I looked up she was just barely smiling at me. I dropped the spatula and walked over to her as she slammed her body into mine.

The way we began kissing each other was like we hadn't seen each other in months. "Brad…oh God…I want…I want…" I was kissing along her neck as she was frantically pulling my boxers off.

"What, baby? What do you want…I'll do whatever you want," I said, panting.

"I want to feel you inside of me...*now*. I want...oh God, I can't believe I'm going to say this."

I pulled back and looked at her. "What? What are you going to say?"

She looked down and then peeked back up to me and said, "I want you to..." she turned her head and looked away as she whispered something. I moved my head forward, straining to hear what it was she was saying.

"Manda, I can't hear you, baby."

She looked back at me and rolled her eyes. "Ugh! Damn it, Ari and Heather said this would be easy!"

I was so confused now. *What in the hell is she talking about?*

"Amanda, you can say anything to me. You know that."

She looked at me, and her eyes changed. I swore they turned gray. "I...um..."

She closed her eyes and when they opened again I almost wanted to suck in a breath of air.

She took a deep breath and said, "I want you to fuck me. Fast and hard."

What? I had to grab onto the counter because my knees buckled at the sound of my wife asking me to fuck her fast and hard.

I couldn't say anything at first, and I saw the fear in her eyes. I moved my hands and placed them on her stomach as she jumped. I slowly moved it down the barely there panties and in one quick move I ripped them off of her. She let out a gasp as I smiled and said, "Oh hell, Manda..." She smiled and bit down on her lip as I motioned for her to turn around with my finger. When she just stood there and smiled I turned her around and pushed her over the table as I moved my hand down and into her. *Shit! She's soaking wet.*

I placed myself right up against her and teased her for a few seconds before I slammed my dick into her from behind. She let out a gasp and said, "Yes! Oh God yes, Brad!" I grabbed onto her hips and began doing just what she asked for. I fucked her fast and hard and did everything I could to hold off.

When I saw her reach her hand down and start touching herself, I had to bite the inside of my cheek to keep from coming.

"Manda...I can't...hold...off...much...more," I panted.

"So close! Ahh...yes...I'm going to come Brad...harder!" She yelled out as I tried to give her what she needed.

I could practically feel her squeezing me as she came and I couldn't hold off any longer. I grabbed her tighter and pumped a few times more as hard as I could before I leaned over her body...overwhelmed with one the most intense orgasms of my life. Trying desperately to catch my breath, I kissed her back and slowly pulled out of her. She turned around and began kissing me. I could hardly breathe, but the way she was kissing me—if I thought I could, I would have taken her again right then.

I pulled back from her and said, "Jesus, where in the hell did that come from?"

She smiled and said, "Oh, it's always been there…I just needed the guts to act on it." I shook my head and laughed. "You never cease to surprise me, do you know that?"

She ran her tongue along the top of her teeth and then scrunched her nose. "I hope not!" She walked over to the stove and turned everything back on before turning back towards me. "The eggs might be dried out a bit but I'm okay with that," she said as she winked, bent down and picked up her panties and walked out of the kitchen. I stood there…half naked… in the kitchen…smiling like an idiot.

I fucking love my wife.

3 Amanda

I stood there and watched Brad fill up the basket with yet more toys from ToysRUs. "Really, Brad?" I looked into the cart and saw an Alphabet Activity Cube, a Laugh and Learn Smart Screen laptop, a LeapFrog Touch Magic counting train, a Walk N Roll rider bike, a little shopper play set, a Disney princess doll, a cell phone with keys and remote control, which I thought Brad got a little too excited about, and a Candy Land game.

"Brad, she can't play Candy Land yet," I said as I put my hands on my hips. My parents were watching Maegan for us while we went shopping, and it was a good thing since we'd been in the store for almost two hours.

"Yeah, but we can play it," Brad said with a smile.

"Why would we *want* to play it?" I asked, giving him a confused look.

He shrugged his shoulders and pushed the cart down another aisle. "Oh no…" I whispered. We were down the baby doll aisle.

"Should we get Alex one?" he asked.

"No! I've bought all the kids their gifts already. No more," I said as I rolled my eyes. But then, I saw the cutest baby doll ever. I quickly glanced at Brad who was looking at one a little too closely. I quickly put four dolls in the cart, one for Alex, Grace, Libby and Maegan. I looked at Brad and started laughing.

"What in the hell are you doing?"

He looked up at me and said, "This thing goes potty. How in the hell does it go potty and why would you want it to go potty?"

I let out a laugh as I walked up, took it out of his hands and put it down.

I grabbed him by the arm and pulled back over to our cart and began pushing it as I said, "Come on, I'm starving, and I need food before I pass out."

I'd never laughed so much as I did with my parents and Brad while we wrapped Christmas presents. Maegan had been exhausted and actually fell asleep before we shut her bedroom door.

"So y'all are leaving in the morning to head to Mason, right?" My mother asked. She had been giving me funny looks all night. Like she wanted to say something to me but didn't know how.

"Yep. Heather and Josh are staying with Jeff and Ari, and we're staying at Gunner and Ells'. It's going to be crazy insane, but I cannot wait," I said. I looked at Brad and he was smiling.

Gunner and Ellie came up with the idea of everyone spending Christmas Day at the ranch. We were telling the kids that Santa left all the presents at Gunner and Ells' place and we would all open gifts there. Then, Heather and Josh were going home to spend Christmas evening with his parents, and we were doing the same with my parents.

"Ellie already has a plan of action of how it's going to go down. Her main thing is that none of the kids are going to be allowed to just rip into gifts. They need to enjoy them, so it's one at a time," Brad said, rolling his eyes.

My mother laughed and said, "That will work for a few years when y'all can control them, but the older they get…they are going to want to rip into the presents."

I let out a giggle. I think next year it's already planned—Christmas morning at our houses and then we will go to Gunner and Ells' place, where the kids will exchange gifts."

"I see. That makes sense because the older they get, the more excited they get, and they want to open gifts first thing," Mom said. She stood up and placed another gift in the box.

I nodded my head and said, "I don't think I could do this every year anyway. Pack up all the gifts and take them to Mason…no way."

"Well…who wants something to snack on? We still have a pile of gifts to wrap!" Mom said. She looked at Brad and raised her eyebrows.

"What? Why are you looking at me? She's just as guilty," Brad said, pointing over at me.

"Yes sweetheart, a snack sounds good. And some hot tea maybe?" my father asked.

"Sure daddy, hot tea it is."

I loved that my parents were here with us. They loved Brad so much and made him feel like he was their son, which was so important to him, especially with his own parents being such asswipes.

We walked into the kitchen and I opened the refrigerator and pulled out some fruit and cheese to make a platter. I spun around to see my mother standing there with her arms crossed over her chest with "the look." I instantly got chills and had to think if I'd done something wrong.

Holy hell, I felt like I was in high school and she was waiting for me to confess I drank alcohol or something.

I looked at her with a confused expression and said, "Umm…something wrong, Mom?"

She just shook her head. *Okay.* "Mom, why are you looking at me like I'm in trouble or something? You're kind of freaking me out…can you stop?"

She smiled and dropped her arms. "Want a glass of wine?" She asked as she moved over to where we kept a few bottles. "Is this the same wine you had the last time I asked for wine?" she asked.

I laughed. "Yep. With Brad not drinking anymore, I just don't really have any of it. I mean I might have one glass if we're out to dinner or something, but I try to stay away from it."

My mother turned and looked at me. "So, do you want me to pour you a glass?" she asked, smiling an evil smile.

"Um…no thanks." Shit. I'm so glad Brad doesn't drink so I can use that as the excuse as to why I don't want anything.

"Oh come on, just one glass. I know for a fact Brad does not care if you have a glass of wine."

She's pure evil. "No thanks," I said with a smile and went back to cutting up fruit.

She let out a sigh and said, "Why not? I just want you to have one glass, Mandy, just one."

Huh? Why is she pushing me? "What? Mom, why is it so important that I have a glass of wine? If you want a glass go ahead. I just don't want one."

"You're a party pooper, come on. I'm going to open up a bottle. Maybe your father will want to join us also."

I slammed the knife on the counter and looked at her. "I. Don't. Want. A. Glass. Of. Wine. Mom."

"Why?"

"Mom!"

"Is it because of the baby?" she whispered.

"Yes! You *know* I can't have any because…" *Oh snap.* I closed my eyes and slowly shook my head. My mother very quietly started jumping up and down and air clapping.

"I knew it! I knew it the moment I saw you," she said in a hushed voice. I watched as she did a goofy dance around the kitchen and I couldn't help but start laughing.

"Really, Mom? How old are you?"

"I'm as old as I feel and I feel like I'm about twenty-five, thank you very much," she said with a wink.

"So?" she asked, then sat on the bar stool and placed her chin on the back of her hand. Her eyes were wide with excitement and she nodded her head like she wanted me to hurry it up.

I shrugged and said, "Sooo…what?"

She dropped her hands and leaned back and just looked at me. "Don't be cute. When did you find out? When are you telling Brad?"

My mouth dropped open. I leaned closer towards her and said, "Is this like some super power older women have? How did you even know and how in the hell do you know I haven't told him yet?"

She took in a deep breath and let it out. "First off, I'd like to say it was a super power but I'm your mother, I just knew the moment I saw you. I could tell. You're glowing. Secondly, Brad told your father earlier that he's getting worried; y'all have been trying to have a baby for a while now. He asked your dad if the drugs he took could be the reason he can't get you pregnant. I overheard them talking and your father assured him that it will happen when it's meant to happen."

I felt the tears stinging my eyes. "Mom…why can't he move past the guilt? I just want him to know how much I love him and that it's all in the past."

She got up and walked around the island. When she took me in her arms, I tried so hard to hold it in but I started crying.

"Oh baby girl, don't cry. I really think this baby is going to help Brad fully heal. I know it will."

I started nodding my head and said, "God, I hope so, Mom. I really hope so. He's doing so good and is so happy and it kills me that he beats himself up over the fact that he missed out on so much of the pregnancy."

She pulled back and gave me a slight smile. "Can you blame him for wanting a second chance?"

Then it hit me like it always does. "But Mom…it's really my fault. I hid the pregnancy from him for so long…maybe if I had told him sooner he might not have gotten so deep…"

She put her fingers up to my lips and shook her head. "No. We don't do this. We don't play the what if's…ever. The past is in the past. Leave it there. If you don't, it will eat you alive and for what? You can't do anything to change it, so learn from it and let it go."

I looked at my mom and smiled. She had always been my rock. She was a therapist and her best friend and colleague had agreed to be Brad's therapist after he got out of rehab. Bryan had suggested that Brad continue to see one for as long as he felt the need. He still goes and talks to her at least twice a month.

Brad walked in and stopped when he saw us. "What's wrong?" he said as he looked at me and then at my mother.

My mom started laughing. "Nothing, sweetheart. I was telling Amanda an old story and she got all emotional." She turned and winked at me as I tried to smile.

Brad walked up and took me into his arms. "I love you," he whispered.

"I love you too."

4 Brad

Christmas Eve

After we had brought all the presents in and put them in the garage, we all headed outside. The girls were all sitting out back laughing and talking.

"What, do the kids all take naps at the same time now?" I asked as I walked up and kissed Amanda on the cheek.

"By some miracle, they all crashed at the same time," Ari said with a chuckle.

"The minute I saw Libby and Will sleeping I just left them where they were…sound asleep in their stroller."

We all let out a soft laugh. Each of the kids had fallen asleep. Ari had been holding a sleeping Grace up until five minutes ago, when she got up and put her in Alex's playpen. Maegan had crashed in the portable playpen a few minutes ago, and Luke was sleeping in one of the lounge chairs.

"Man, Luke looks like his dad after a night of heavy drinking," I said as I punched Jeff in the arm.

"Fuck you, dude."

I looked around at everyone and then shook my head.

"I wish Scott and Jessie were here," I said, and everyone nodded in agreement.

Ellie let out a small sigh and then said, "Okay. So everyone knows the game plan right? Y'all are all going to come over around eight in the morning, right?"

Ari and Heather moaned as Ellie gave them a look. "I know your kids are up by then, so don't moan about it. If we start early that gives us all time to hang out and then get ready to spend the afternoon with our parents."

"Fine, but if Luke sleeps in, my ass is letting him. He's a monster if you wake him up before he's ready," Ari said as Jeff laughed and agreed.

We spent the next hour or so talking and laughing about everything and nothing. Ellie talked about the baby and how excited she was, Josh talked about how well the business was going and how he just landed a huge job for a doctor's office in Fredericksburg, and Jeff and Gunner talked about the ranch.

I had yet to tell Amanda I got a promotion at work and that I was now going to be able to work from home most of the time. I couldn't wait to tell her and planned on telling her tonight sometime. I loved spending every single minute with her and Meg, so this was perfect. I didn't even care when she dragged me to all those craft shows and into all the stores in Fredericksburg, even though we'd been in them a thousand times. I just loved being with her. As we all enjoyed the rest of the afternoon, I couldn't help but feel more and more excited about telling Amanda the good news.

Gunner and I sat on the back porch that evening and talked after I had helped Amanda put Maegan down to bed. I was surprised Meg went to sleep in the portable crib so well in our room. She was a creature of habit and usually didn't take too well to change. I looked up to see Amanda and Ellie walk out onto the porch. Amanda looked at me and her cheeks instantly blushed. I couldn't help but wonder what she had been thinking of to 'cause her to blush like that. Maybe the other morning in the kitchen perhaps. I had to move and adjust my jeans just thinking about that morning. *Damn.*

She walked over and sat down in my lap. She moved a little and must have felt my hard on, because she raised her eyebrows and winked.

"Want to go for a walk?" she asked.

I looked out into the dark night and smiled. "Baby, it's pitch dark out."

She held up two flashlights and winked.

I let out a laugh and said, "My baby wants to go on a midnight stroll, let's go for a stroll."

She jumped up and let out a little shriek and so did Ellie. Gunner smiled and shrugged his shoulders. Ellie handed a blanket to Amanda and she wrapped it around her shoulders. She had on a sweatshirt, so I couldn't believe she was still cold.

"You want a heavier jacket so you don't have to carry the blanket?" I asked as Gunner stood up.

"No!" Ellie and Amanda both yelled. I took a step back and held up my hands. "Okay. Okay…blanket it is." Gunner threw his head back and laughed.

"Why do I think this was planned?" he said as he looked over at a smiling Ellie.

She slowly shook her head and said, "I don't know what you mean."

Amanda giggled as she hooked her arm in mine and we headed off for our stroll in the dark. As we walked, Amanda took in a deep breath of air.

"God, I love it out here," she said as she put her head back some.

My heart started beating faster. Now with my promotion, we could move closer to everyone since I would be working from home mostly.

"Yeah, I do too. Would you ever want to move out here?" I asked, trying to be as casual as I could.

Even though I couldn't see her face, I could tell she was smiling. "In a heartbeat—if I didn't think you would have to get an apartment and live in Austin and come home on the weekends!"

We both laughed and she reached down and took my hand. I was letting her lead the way since she had a clear plan of where we were going.

"Are we going to the barn?" I asked.

She didn't say anything and picked up the pace a bit.

"What's the rush, pumpkin? Where in the hell are you trying to go?"

She squeezed my hand and said, "The barn, damn it, but I just heard something running off! Hurry and walk faster!"

I reached down and swept her off her feet, carrying her the rest of the way to the barn. Gunner had built it right after his house was done and they only kept a few horses out there. It was probably the nicest barn I'd ever seen. The upper loft was finished out and a few times me, Gunner, Jeff and Josh had gone up there and just sat for hours shooting the shit. *Fuck. I want to move out here and be closer to our friends.*

The moment we walked into the barn and I saw the light coming from upstairs I knew something was up. I looked at Amanda and winked.

"You had this planned all along?" I asked her as I slowly set her down.

She nodded her head and bit down on her lower lip and started chewing on it. *Clear sign she's nervous about something.* She slowly started walking backwards and over to the stairs. *She didn't want to…here? In Gunner's barn?*

I let out a small chuckle and started to follow her before I stopped. "Amanda…are you really wanting to have sex in Gunner's barn? Baby, I love this new side of you and all, but…" I turned back and looked at the opening to the barn.

When I turned back around she was halfway up the stairs. Then I heard her let out a gasp and I took off up the stairs after her.

"What? What's wrong…what did you—" I stopped dead in my tracks. "Oh wow," I whispered. The loft was covered in white lights. Everywhere you looked were lights. The small round table that was up here was covered in a beautiful white tablecloth and there was a huge bouquet of white roses. As I followed Amanda, I noticed there was a tray of chocolate-covered strawberries and another tray that had fruit and cheese on it. Next to the table was a bottle of sparkling water and I had to laugh. I think I was the only one out of our friends who no longer drank. The two glasses on the table said "Congratulations" on them.

Holy hell. How did Amanda find out about my promotion?

Amanda put her hands up to her mouth and started crying. Why is she crying about my promotion? I thought she'd be happy. Shit.

I walked up behind her and wrapped my arms around her and asked, "Why are you crying?"

She slowly nodded her head and said, "They made it so special. They did this for us." Then she began sobbing. I turned her around and pulled her chin up and looked into her eyes.

"Who made it so special?"

She wiped her nose in a not-so-romantic way and laughed. "Ari, Heather, Ellie and Jen. They planned all this for us."

I shook my head. "How did they find out?"

She looked at me with a shocked expression. "What? How did they find out what?"

"That I got promoted at work?" I said. Amanda looked even more confused.

"You got promoted at work?" she asked, her mouth dropping open and her eyes lighting up.

I nodded my head. "Yep. I'm now going to be working mostly from home—

except for when I have to go in for meetings where they need me there."

She slammed her hands over her mouth and started jumping up and down. "Oh. My. God! You're going to be home with Meg and me? All the time?"

I nodded my head and she immediately fell into my arms and began crying harder.

"Thank you God. Oh…my…oh thank you, thank you, thank you," she whispered in between sobs.

Now I was the one who was confused. I thought she knew about the promotion. I pulled her away from me and said, "Wait. I thought you knew about the promotion."

She shook her head quickly. "No! How would I know about it? I didn't think they were announcing it until after the first of the year. Oh, Brad. This is such wonderful news!" She went to hug me again but I stopped her.

I shook my head to clear my thoughts. "Wait, pumpkin…if you didn't know about the promotion, what is this all about?" I looked at the crystal glasses. "I mean the glasses say "Congratulations" on them. What else are we celebrating?"

She bit down on her lip and began chewing on it again. I pulled it out and said, "Manda, stop chewing your lip off."

"Sorry…um…well…um…" She looked into my eyes, and I swore the look in her eyes took my breath away. She reached into her back pocket and had something wrapped in a piece of Christmas tissue. She went to hand it to me but then stopped.

"I wanted to give you your Christmas present tonight. Alone. I asked the girls to help me come up with something and well…" she looked around and let out a chuckle. "They certainly helped me come up with something."

She looked into my eyes and again as she handed me the tissue paper.

"Merry Christmas, baby. I love you," she whispered.

I took the tissue paper from her and smiled. It was light as a feather. "Is there even anything in here? I asked.

She nodded and said, "Oh yeah."

I started to open it up and unwrap it and that's when I saw it.

Oh my God. It's a pregnancy test.

I quickly looked at her and immediately felt the tears building in my eyes. I glanced back down and turned the test around.

I felt my legs starting to shake as I looked back up at her. She was crying and I was barely able to even say a word.

I whispered, "We're pregnant?"

She slowly nodded her head and I dropped to the ground and began crying.

The next thing I knew she was on the ground with me, crying just as hard as I was. I got on my knees and pulled her to me and held onto her as tight as I could.

The only thing I could say was, "Thank you God…thank you God…" over and over. *I get my second chance. I finally get my second chance.*

I pulled back and quickly wiped away my tears, and then wiped Amanda's away with my thumbs.

"I just found out two days ago. I wanted to make it special for you. That's why I waited to tell you, even though I wanted to tell you so badly. I wanted to make it special for you," she said as she began crying again. I placed my hands on her face and brought her lips to mine.

"I love you…my God, I love you so much," I said as I kissed her with as much passion and love as I could. *She did this for me. My God, this amazing woman did this for me.*

"I love you too, Brad. I love you so very much." She said as she pulled back from my lips.

I slowly shook my head. "I don't deserve you." She put her hand behind my neck and pulled me into another kiss. I could literally feel her love pouring into my body and I'd never felt so at peace in my entire life.

She started to stand up and I followed her. She looked up into my eyes and said, "Yes. Yes you do deserve me, like I deserve you. We were meant to be together Brad. For always. Nothing will ever come between our love…ever."

I ran the back of my hand softly across her cheek. "You're so beautiful. I knew something was different about you the other night…you were…you were glowing."

She smiled and closed her eyes. I looked up and couldn't believe what I saw. *A bed? When in the hell did Gunner put a bed up here and why?*

Amanda turned and looked and started laughing. "You are probably wondering why there is a bed up here."

"Well, yeah I can't deny I'm at a loss. And it's a damn nice bed at that."

Amanda turned back to look at me. "Gunner wanted a little place for him and Ells to sneak off to sometimes to keep things romantic. He had Josh build it and they must have put it in recently."

I closed my eyes and laughed. "Damn. That boy is such a romantic son of a bitch."

Amanda laughed. "When Ellie mentioned it to me earlier, I had to laugh. Then I said Gunner wasn't going to be too happy about that bed being here when his kids get older."

I threw my head back and laughed my ass off. "Ah hell…brings new meaning to sneaking off to the barn to make out!"

Once we stopped laughing, Amanda grabbed the blanket and started to walk over to the bed. It had a quilt on it already, but Amanda threw the blanket on top of it and then turned to face me. The moment she began undressing I wanted to fall to the floor. I was about to make love to my wife…and she's pregnant with our child. My heart was bursting with joy.

I watched as she took everything off and stood there. I looked her body up and down and then began to take my clothes off. The chill in the air wasn't even noticeable…I was breathing so hard and Amanda's chest was heaving up and down, turning me on even more. Once I was finished undressing, I walked over to her and stopped right in front of her. I took the back of my hand and ran it down from her face all the way to her stomach. When I touched her, she sucked in a breath of air and I smiled when I remembered her doing the same thing the other night.

"Amanda…"

She slowly sat on the bed and then lay down. I moved and hovered over her body. I felt the tears building and she smiled as she leaned up and kissed one away.

"Brad, please don't cry."

I smiled and brought my lips to hers as I gently kissed her. "I get to make love to you…while you're pregnant with our child."

She giggled and said, "You've been making love to me the last few weeks and I've been pregnant."

I shook my head and closed my eyes thinking back to the last few weeks of being with her. Every time I'm with Amanda it feels like the first time. "No…this time is different." I moved closer to her and then I slowly entered her body.

"God Amanda…I don't ever want to leave this moment…ever."

She gently ran her fingertips up and down my skin, and I felt goose bumps cover my whole body.

"Kiss me, Brad," she whispered.

I slowly began moving my lips along her neck and up to her lips. I kissed her slowly, passionately and for what seemed like forever.

I took my time making love to her. I wanted her to feel every emotion I was feeling.

Once we were done making love, I lay there and held her in my arms. Moving my fingers up and down her arm, I took in a deep breath and slowly let it out.

"What are you thinking about?" Amanda asked me in a sleepy voice.

I smiled and said, "You."

She looked up at me and put her chin on my chest and smiled. "Me? What about me?"

"You know…the usual stuff. How much I love you. How wonderful of a mother you are. How you're such an amazing wife. How you love me and believe in me. How you never gave up on me and walked away when I gave you so many reasons to." My voice cracked at the end and I closed my eyes to keep myself from crying like the pussy I was.

She slowly got up and crawled on top of me. I put my hands on her hips and looked at her beautiful face.

"Do you know why I'm all those things?" she asked as I shook my head.

"Because of your love and because *you* believe in *me*. I couldn't imagine my life without you in it, Brad. I wouldn't ever want to. I love you so much. Please don't ever doubt that or doubt our love."

I sat up and put my hand behind her neck as I began to bring her lips to mine.

"I never would. Ever."

5 Amanda

Christmas Day

I opened my eyes, stretched and smiled. I'd never felt so wonderful in my life. I smiled as I thought about last night in Gunner and Ellie's barn. I brought my fingers up to my lips and gently ran them back and forth over my still kiss-swollen lips.

I looked to my left and Brad was gone. I sat up and glanced over at the portable crib and Maegan was not in there. I slowly got out of bed and made my way into the bathroom. I let out a gasp as I saw the vase of roses sitting on the sink. I quickly looked all around me and laughed.

"How?" I said as I walked up and smelled them. I brushed my teeth and changed as I made my way downstairs. I heard Ellie and Brad talking in the kitchen. When I walked into the kitchen, they both stopped talking as they looked at me with big goofy-ass grins on their faces. I looked at both girls sitting in high chairs eating. I couldn't help but smile at the sight.

"Merry Christmas sleepy head!" Ellie said as she walked over to me and gave me a hug.

I hugged her back and looked at the stove. "Jesus, what time did you get up? I've never seen so many things cooking at one time!"

Ellie looked back at the stove and laughed. "Gunner wanted to have a big ole Southern Christmas breakfast. Everyone should be showing up any second!"

I looked around and saw biscuits, gravy, blueberry muffins, sausage and egg casserole, glazed apples, French toast, pancakes, bacon, grits and ham, and even more items were in both ovens.

"Holy hell. What time did you wake up? Why didn't you wake me up to help?" I asked. I finally noticed Brad wearing a Christmas apron.

"I got up at five and then Brad came down and ran an errand and came back and helped."

I peeked over at my husband, who was mixing something in a bowl. He winked at me and smiled.

"The flowers?" I asked.

"Did you like them?" he asked, with that smile that melts my heart.

I walked over and gave him a kiss and whispered against his lips, "Yes. I loved them. Thank you."

"Merry Christmas, pumpkin," he said with a wink.

"Merry Christmas, Brad."

I turned to Alex and Maegan and clapped my hands and smiled. "Merry Christmas to two of the most beautiful girls in the whole world!"

They both laughed and Maegan smeared more oatmeal in her hair as Alex shoveled in her oatmeal. I couldn't help but laugh.

Before I knew it, the house was filled. The guys all had the kids while the girls all got breakfast ready. I'd never laughed so hard in my life. Every now and then I would peek out and check on the guys. Brad looked like he was walking on cloud nine. If I didn't know any better, I would think he had the same pregnancy glow I did.

"So? How was last night?" Heather asked, while Ari wiggled her eyebrows up and down.

I leaned against the counter and fanned myself as they all started laughing. "I'm telling you, pregnancy sex is the best kind of sex. They need to bottle that shit up and sell it," Ari said as she pulled more biscuits out of the oven.

Emma, Sharon, and Grace were setting the table in the formal dinning room and the breakfast area. Emma was walking through the kitchen as she said, "It sure is the best kind of sex."

We all stopped talking and just looked at her. When she rounded the corner, we all snapped our heads over to look at Ellie. She smiled and held up her hands and laughed. "Hey…don't look at me."

Ari busted out laughing and then whispered, "I'm telling y'all…I totally think Emma and Garrett still sneak off and get them some in the barn." .

"Oh God! Please, Ari, don't even go there," Ellie said as she attempted to clear the image from her head.

We all sat down and started breakfast. There was so many conversations going on I couldn't help but sit back and just enjoy it all. I looked around at everyone, eating, laughing, telling jokes and reminiscing on Christmases past.

Gunner stood up and got everyone's attention, "Okay, first, thank you to my beautiful bride and all the ladies who whipped up this amazing breakfast. I've never seen so much food in my life." Everyone agreed and Ellie thanked everyone for pitching in and helping.

"Now, let's all head into the family room and do what we've all been waiting for…open Christmas presents for the kids!"

Everyone laughed and started to stand up.

"Clean-up duty is on the guys, and I vote for taking care of it after a bit of fun," Gunner called out.

Jeff, Josh and Brad all agreed as we made our way into the family room.

I sat down on the floor over by the fireplace and Brad sat down next to me and put Maegan in his lap. The Christmas music in the background added just the perfect touch to the whole scene.

Gunner and Ellie had a huge seven-and-a-half foot live Christmas tree that was decorated in all silver, white and red ornaments with white lights. It was breathtaking. There was a smaller tree in the formal living room that had all their "fun" ornaments on it. Ellie smiled when she said that would be the tree the kids would decorate, but the main tree would always be her tree. Gunner rolled his eyes and brought her in for a kiss.

I laughed because Brad and I had a hodge-podge of a tree. It was covered in ornaments from both our childhoods and ornaments from trips we had taken. Everywhere we went, we tried to find an ornament for our collection.

"Ellie would pass out if she saw our tree!" Brad whispered.

I giggled and said, "And just think if she knew we had multicolored lights on it."

Brad tossed his head back and laughed.

I wasn't sure how we kept order with all the presents being passed around. Luke was probably having the most fun with ripping open his and Grace's gifts. Gunner was walking around with a large trash bag collecting all the wrapping paper, while Alex attempted to help him.

Maegan was sitting in a walker that Ellie, Heather and Ari bought her. She was mesmerized by it. Brad leaned over and said, "Damn...we can put Meg in that and sneak in a little play time!"

I nodded my head and smiled.

By the time the guys had made their way back to the dining room and kitchen, I was holding a sleeping Maegan.

"Ells, I'm going to go upstairs and put Maegan down."

Ellie nodded her head and winked at me.

Right after I put Maegan in the portable crib, I felt someone put his hands on my hips. I jumped and spun around. I didn't even have time to think before Brad's lips were on mine. He began reaching up under my shirt with one hand as he tried unbuttoning my jeans with his other hand.

I pushed him away and looked at him. "Brad! What in the world are you doing? Everyone is downstairs."

He smiled that smile of his and pulled me back to him. He began kissing my neck and moved his lips over to my ear. *Oh. God. I loved when he did that.*

His hot breath was on my neck as he whispered in my ear, "I want you, Manda."

Gah...I wanted him so badly I could hardly stand it. "Brad," I whispered. "We can't."

He picked me up and I wrapped my legs around him as he walked into the bathroom and shut the door. He pushed me against the wall and began kissing me passionately. *God…what was happening to me?*

"Brad…yes…" I whispered. He gently set me down, and the next thing I knew we were both taking our clothes off faster than ever. Brad stood there and looked my body up and down as he licked his lips.

"Oh God…Brad…" He moved closer to me as he reached behind my neck and pulled me to him. He began kissing me and he let out one small deep moan after another.

"Amanda…" he whispered against my lips. He picked me up and gently moved me down until I felt him buried inside me. He walked me back up against the wall and slowly started to move in and out.

I needed more.

"Faster," I whispered. "Harder."

He pulled back and looked at me as he gave me a wicked smile. He lifted me up off of him and I instantly missed him. He set me down and glanced over toward the tub.

"Put your hands on the tub baby." *Oh. My. God.* I walked over and did as he asked. Before I knew it he was inside me again going fast and hard. It felt like heaven and I didn't want it to stop. I had to really concentrate on not calling out when my orgasm hit.

"Baby…I'm gonna come," Brad whispered.

I swore I felt him coming inside of me.

Then, there was a knock on the bedroom door. Brad instantly pulled out of me and started getting dressed. I turned around…still trying to get my body to come down from my orgasm. I couldn't help it, but I had to start laughing as I watched Brad scramble around trying to get dressed. He looked at me and threw my clothes at me and said, "Shit! Get dressed!" He opened the bathroom door and shut it.

I started getting dressed as I heard him talking to someone. I stopped and walked over to the bathroom to hear who he was talking to. I put my hand up to my mouth and tried like hell to hold my laugh in.

Garrett! He really did have some kind of radar.

I quickly got dressed, fixed my just-fucked hair and waited until they both left. I opened the door and checked on my sleeping beauty, still peacefully asleep.

As I made my way downstairs, I saw Ari and Ellie looking at me. They both busted out laughing and I gave them the finger. I made my way over to where they were standing. As I walked up to them, Heather grabbed my arm and pulled me off to the side while Ari and Ellie followed.

One look at each other we all busted out laughing. "I guess he really does have some kind of superpower to tell when two people are having sex," I whispered.

"Oh. My. God. That makes all of us he's interrupted," Ellie said as she giggled.

"I tell ya what. I've never seen Brad get dressed so damn fast in my life!"

We all started laughing again. "Be glad you don't live close by. There is a very good reason we have double locks on our doors," Ari whispered.

Then Ellie put her hands on her hips and looked at me. "Oh my God. I can't believe you had sex, Amanda! Everyone is here!"

I felt my cheeks blush as Ari pushed Ellie. "Shit, you're just jealous because your ass can't sneak of with Gunner and get your nasty on."

Ellie smiled and nodded her head. "I am!"

"So?" Heather asked as she wiggled her eyebrows up and down.

All three of them leaned in closer to me. They were staring at me like I was about to share something earth-shattering.

"So? What?" I asked.

Ari rolled her eyes. "How was it? Did it make it hotter knowing that y'all were sneaking in a quickie with everyone down here?"

I looked around quickly as I felt my cheeks burn. I bit down on my lip and turned back to look at my three best friends.

"It was *very* hot," I whispered. All three of them let out squeals.

"Shit…don't tell me where you had sex…I don't want to know," Ellie said.

"Fuck, I do!" Ari said. "I bet it was in the bathroom since Meg was in the bedroom."

Heather nodded her head. "I'm going to guess it was from behind too."

My mouth dropped open as I looked between Heather and Ari.

"What the fuck. Did you have a camera in there?" I said as I gave them both a shocked look.

They both started laughing. "I'm just thinking that is what Jeff and I would do," Ari said with a wink.

"Ewww!" Ellie said.

I let out a giggle.

"Clearly Gunner and I need to try something different," Ellie said. Heather and Ari both snapped their heads over at her.

"Oh my God, really? Because I've been dying to give you this kit…" Ari started rattling off.

Ellie blushed and said, "Um…I don't think I'll be needing your kit, Ari." She winked at Heather who jumped up and down.

"You bought it?" Heather asked.

Ellie nodded her head.

"Wait! Bought what? What did you buy!" Ari and I both said at the same time.

Ellie pursed her lips and tilted her head. "Oh…just a little sex kit from Lelo."

"Jesus H. Christ. Finally!" Ari said as she gave a little fist pump.

I let out a laugh. "Did you give it to him yet?"

Ellie shook her head. "Nope. We are exchanging gifts tonight. I have a feeling what Gunner bought is something he wants me to see after everyone is gone and Alex is in bed.

Heather leaned back against the wall. "God, I love Christmas."

As we stood there laughing and discussing Ellie's new adventure, Emma came walking up and we all stopped talking.

"Now girls, you don't have to stop talking sex just because an older woman walks up. I might actually have some tips for you," she said with a wink.

We all looked at each other and I was pretty sure Ellie was about to throw up.

"I just don't even know what to say to that, Emma," Ellie whispered.

Emma threw her head back and laughed.

"Emma, what was it like for you? I mean, when you first met Garrett…was it love at first sight?" Heather asked with a huge grin on her face.

The smile that spread across Emma's face almost caused me to suck in a breath of air. You could almost see it on her face…feel it in the air…her love for Garrett.

She shook her head and gave a slight chuckle. "Oh girls…I don't think I could even put it in words what I felt the first time I laid eyes on Garrett Mathews. My heart literally stopped. All he did was smile at me and his smile about knocked me over. Then I saw his eyes." She began fanning herself with her hand as she giggled. "Damn those eyes. If I hadn't known any better I would have thought he looked into my soul and captured my love on the spot."

"Oh, how romantic," Ellie purred.

"Was Garrett romantic like the overly romantic-ass Gunner?" Ari asked with a wink toward Ellie.

Emma let out a laugh. "Oh yes. But, I was stubborn. Very stubborn and I refused to let him for the longest time."

"Why?" we all asked at once.

"Girls, it was so long ago and it's such a long story. Garrett and I will have to sit down one day and tell y'all our story."

We all nodded our heads like little kids being told they were going to get candy soon.

"That would be amazing, Emma! I've always wanted to know how y'all fell in love," I said as I put my hand to my heart.

Ari let out a gruff laugh and said, "Shit. What I want to know is did Garrett's grandfather have a sixth sense and knew when y'all were getting it on and interrupt your asses!"

Everyone snapped their heads over and looked at Ari and then busted out laughing.

Including Emma.

6 Brad

I sat back and watched Gunner and Jeff swinging Ellie and Ari around as they danced to "Jingle Bell Rock" by Blake Shelton. Amanda was holding Maegan and dancing and Meg was laughing so hard at how Amanda was bouncing her around.

I'd never been so damn happy in my life. I watched them both and was captivated by their smiles. Amanda looked beautiful and the glow on her face made my stomach drop.

I felt someone come up behind me and give me a light tap on the back. I turned to see Josh sitting down.

"I don't think I've seen you smile more than I have this morning, dude," he said with a small laugh.

I let out a small chuckle and nodded my head. "I don't think I've ever been this happy before. I can't even begin to tell you how happy I am about Amanda being pregnant."

I glanced at Josh who was watching Amanda dancing with Meg. He smiled and said, "I'm really proud of you, Brad."

My mouth dropped open as I continued to look at him. "Why?"

He turned to look at me and winked. "Brad, you stood up against something that could have very well have knocked you down and kept you there. You fought like hell to get your life back. I see how you look at Amanda and I know for a fact you've never looked at another woman the way you look at her. I see you with Meg and I only hope that I'm half as good of a father as you are. You put them both first and I think that says something about you as a man, a father and a husband as well."

I felt the tears building in my eyes. I couldn't believe what I was hearing. I'd always looked up to Josh. He always seemed to have his shit together and he knew from the beginning what he was going to do with his life.

"Josh, I can't even begin to tell you how this makes me feel to hear you say those things to me. You of all people. Dude, you're an amazing father. I mean…" I looked back out at Heather. She was holding Libby, and the smile on her face was unreal as she danced around with Amanda and Meg to "Santa Claus Is Coming to Town." "Look at Heather, Josh." Josh glanced back out to where they were dancing and he smiled. "That smile on her face says it all."

He nodded and let out a laugh. "I guess we're all lucky sons of bitches, aren't we?"

"Hell yeah we are. Best damn Christmas of my life," I said.

Nat King Cole's "O Come All Ye Faithful" was playing on the radio, as Amanda and Maegan were fast asleep in the car. I smiled to myself thinking about how much fun it was to spend Christmas morning and afternoon with all of our friends. Ellie mentioned how it wouldn't work once the kids were older. "They'll never be able to hold out on opening presents," she said. Then Gunner said, "Hell, I won't be able to hold out."

As I came around the corner, I saw a BMW sitting in our driveway.

"Fuck," I whispered as I saw my mother and father talking to our neighbors. A part of me wanted to drive right on by and not even stop. They had never even seen Maegan and I wanted to keep it that way. After the things my mother said to Amanda, there was no way I could ever forgive her. *Ever.*

Then Larry pointed to my truck. *Son of a bitch.* I slowed down and pulled in the driveway and opened the garage door. As I pulled in oh so slowly so as to not wake Amanda, I looked over and said a prayer that they would both stay asleep. I quietly got out of the truck and gently shut the door.

I took a deep breath and walked over to where my parents were standing. Larry was still talking to them and he gave me a funny look.

"Brad, darling!" My mother said as she started to walk toward me. I put my hand up and she stopped instantly. My father walked up and held out his hand. I reached out and shook it. "Dad."

"Merry Christmas, son," he said with a weak smile. I knew my father was caught in the middle and I also knew he really liked Amanda.

My mother looked disappointed. She glanced over my shoulder and looked at the truck. "Where are Amanda and the baby?"

I turned and looked at my truck and then looked back at her. "They're asleep in the truck."

"Where were y'all?" she said with a questioning look. "Amanda's parents' house?"

"No, Mom. They'll be here soon though."

She just looked at me. "So?"

I shrugged my shoulders. "So what?"

"Well, son, where were y'all? We came to bring the baby her presents."

My mother and father didn't even know the name of their only grandchild.

"Maegan. Her name is Maegan, Mom."

My mother smiled slightly. "Oh…I guess that is a good name."

My father snapped his head over and looked at my mother

I shook my head. *She'll never change.* "We were in Mason, celebrating Christmas with our friends. What are you doing here?"

With that, Larry quickly turned and walked back into his house. I was sure he'd be asking questions later.

My mother squared off her shoulders. "I came to see my grandchild and son and give them their Christmas presents." *Bitch.* Did she think I didn't notice how she didn't mention Amanda?

"I'm sorry you made the trip out here for nothing."

She looked confused and glanced over to my father before looking back at me and giving me that look that used to make me cringe, but no longer had an effect on me.

"I'm sorry? What do you mean 'for nothing?' " she asked.

"I mean, I don't want anything from you, and neither does our daughter. Yes, *our* daughter, Mom. Just because you don't say her name doesn't mean that Amanda is not very much a part of my world."

She rolled her eyes. "Oh, for Pete's sake. You're mad because I didn't say Amanda's name. Fine. We have presents, for you, our grandchild and your wife…Amanda."

"Please leave, Mom, and don't ever come back." I gave my father a quick look, and his eyes were filled with sadness. I went to turn away from them when my mother grabbed my arm.

"Bradley. This has gone on too long. How long are you going to punish us? We want to see our grandchild. We deserve to see her, damn it."

I let out laugh and shook my head. "You tried to destroy my marriage, Mom. You threatened me and wanted me to leave my wife. I'm sorry…I have nothing left to say to you, and yes…before you even say it, I will always put my wife first. *Always.* I love her more than I could ever describe. She is my whole world, as well as Maegan and the baby. I'll never let you hurt any of them."

My mother put her hand up to her mouth. "Oh…is Amanda pregnant?"

I looked at her with a confused expression on my face. "What? Why would you ask that?"

"You said Maegan and the baby, son," my father said.

Fuck me.

"Um…" I said, trying to figure out how to dig myself out of this one.

My mother let out a gasp as she looked over my shoulder, and I spun around. Amanda was standing there holding Maegan. Maegan was just staring at my mother and father.

"She's beautiful," my mother whispered.

When I looked back at my mother, she had tears running down her face.

Amanda walked up to me and I put my arm around her. I swore I felt her body tremble. There was no way I was going to ever let my mother hurt her again.

My father walked up and smiled at Amanda and she returned the smile. "She's breathtaking, Amanda." He said as he smiled down at Maegan, who reached out for him with her hand. He took her hand and kissed it as she buried her face in Amanda's neck.

I watched as my father talked to Maegan, and my heart broke into a million pieces. I peeked over at my mother and watched her face as my father talked to my daughter. When he stepped back, he looked at my mother. Before she took a step closer, she looked at Amanda.

"May I?" she asked.

Amanda nodded her head and took a step closer to my mother.

"Hello, Maegan. My goodness, you are the spitting image of your daddy," my mother said as I watched a tear slide down her cheek. My heart was pounding in my chest.

Amanda looked up at me and smiled. "I told Brad she looked like him."

My mother looked right at Amanda and giggled. "I'll have to give you some baby pictures, the resemblance is unbelievable."

"I'd really like that," Amanda said as her voice choked.

What happened next really surprised me and took my breath away. My mother put her hand up to her mouth and started crying as she looked at Amanda and placed her hand on Amanda's face.

"Oh my God. I'm so sorry…I'm so very sorry for treating you so horribly." She turned and walked into my father's arms. He held her while he stroked his hand down her back and kept saying, "Shh…baby. Shh…"

Amanda looked at me with a stunned look on her face. I was just as stunned and didn't really know what to do. Amanda motioned for me to invite them into the house but I shook my head no. She tilted her head and gave me another look. She mouthed 'Brad' to me and I rolled my eyes. The last thing I wanted to do was open it up for her to hurt Amanda more.

I took in a deep breath and quickly let it out. "Dad, did y'all want to, um, come in for a bit?"

My father pushed my mother away and looked at her. He looked back up at me and said, "I think your mother and I would really like that."

My mom spun around, quickly wiping her eyes and putting on a smile. "I'd love to be able to get those pictures to you…" her voice cracked.

Amanda nodded her head. "Of course, please just let me know when and maybe we can meet y'all for lunch sometime."

The expression on my mom's face was pure shock.

She began shaking her head. "Why? Why would you be so nice to me after all of the horrible things I did to you?"

I glanced down at my beautiful wife. I knew why, because that was just Amanda. She didn't have a mean bone in her body, but at the same time, she was very guarded and I trusted that she knew what she was doing.

"It does me no good to hang on to hurt and anger. Will I ever be able to forgive you? Yes. Forgetting is hard, but I'm willing to give it a try." She glanced up at me and smiled. "For Brad, because I love him and I know he loves his parents and I know Maegan will want to know her grandparents. So will the new baby."

My mother dropped her head and then looked back up. The tears were flowing and a part of me wanted to take her into my arms.

She quickly wiped away the tears and smiled. "Okay, well. We have presents…for each of you," she said as she looked at me and winked. I had to wonder if they did have presents for Amanda. When my father opened up the trunk of their car, Maegan started clapping and smiling. She somehow knew that what she was looking at would surely mean lots of fun for her.

I helped my parents carry the more than ridiculous amount of presents as we put them under the tree. I couldn't help but notice that there were about six presents with Amanda's name on them. I glanced over at my mother, who was now holding Maegan. For some reason I got the idea that deep down inside, she liked Amanda. She was just too stubborn to admit it.

The afternoon went on as my mother played endlessly with Maegan and my parents chatted with Amanda's parents. We had waited for Amanda's parents to get there before we opened up presents and poor Maegan could hardly keep her eyes open from all the excitement of the day.

I stood over Maegan's crib, watching her sleep. Amanda grabbed my hand and I turned to around to face her. The smile on her face about blew me over.

"Are you happy?" she whispered.

I brought her in for a hug and held her tightly against my body. "I've never had such an amazing Christmas before."

As we walked into the hallway I could hear my parents talking to Amanda's. I was pleasantly surprised at how well everyone seemed to be getting along.

"I love you, Manda. I love you because I know you stepping out of my truck and walking up to my parents with Meg had to have been hard for you. Especially with everything my mother said to you."

She got up on her tippy toes and kissed me. "I love you. And I see how guarded you've been this afternoon. You have to admit it was nice seeing your parents playing with Meg. Didn't you think so?"

As much as I wanted to admit I loved having my parents here, I was still angry at my mother.

"Brad, let it go. Baby, let the anger and hurt go. We have so much to look forward to and what is in the past is in the past."

I shook my head. "Manda, how can you say that after the things she put you through? She put us through? She said some horrible things and I'm...I'm just not sure I can forgive her."

She slipped her hand behind my neck and brought my lips down to hers. She gently kissed me as she moved her hand through my hair. She stopped kissing me and barely took her lips from mine.

"I can forgive her because of this. Our love, Brad. Our love is so much stronger than any words she can spit out, and I really, truly honestly believe that she didn't mean it. I think you were her baby, and no matter who your wife was...she just had it set in her mind they were not good enough. I think the moment she saw Meg it all hit her. She's missed out on so much and I don't think she wants to miss out on any more."

I took a deep breath in and slowly blew it out as I closed my eyes.

"Listen, I'm not saying let's have your parents over for dinners and tea parties, but let's try and let them be a part of our lives. A part of our children's lives. We'll just take it one day at a time. How does that sound?" She scrunched up her nose and winked at me and I couldn't help but let out a chuckle.

"I don't think they will be trying to come over and bother us too much, especially after we move."

"Yeah I don't think so...huh? What do you mean? After we move?"

"I think it's time for me to give you your Christmas present. I was waiting for the parents to all leave but seeing as they are all catching up and shit, I'll just have to give it to you now...I could care less if they're here or not."

She smiled and nodded her head like a little girl. "Oh wait! Is it something sexual? I'll wait if it is!"

I laughed as I put my arm around her as we began walking to the living room.

"No baby...well, at least your big present isn't. The other present is going to have to wait until they are gone for sure though."

She let out a gasp and gave me that smile of hers that reminds me each time I see it how much I love her.

Oh yeah…I wasn't sure which present I was looking forward to giving her more. *That's a lie.* I knew which one I was looking forward to giving her, and I was going to do everything in my power to get everyone out of my house within the next fifteen minutes.

7   Amanda

As we made our way into the living room, I caught my mother looking at me. She gave me a slight smile. I knew she was being friendly to Brad's mother for the sake of Brad. I had to pull her aside before they walked in to tell her not go crazy ape on her.

I gave her a look that said *time to leave now*, and she nodded her head.

"Well, I'm exhausted and know Manda and Brad have had a long day. I think we'll take off. Forty-five minute drive back home and all," my mother said as she winked at my father.

I walked up to her and hugged her. "Thank you, Mom, so much for coming over and spending Christmas with us. It meant a lot to me," I whispered in her ear. "Thank you for holding your tongue too!"

She pulled away and winked at me.

"I guess we better head on out as well. I know you're both tired," Carol said. Brad reached over and gave his mother a hug good-bye, but quickly stepped away before she could lean in for a kiss. I saw disappointment etched all over her face. He shook his father's hand and turned to lead everyone out.

When we walked back in, we both collapsed onto the sofa.

"Motherfucker, that was emotionally exhausting," I said as I peeked over at Brad. He had his eyes closed but nodded his head. Then he snapped his head over to me and gave me the biggest panty-melting smile I'd ever seen. I swore I was wet between my legs within seconds.

"Your gift," he said, in the sexiest damn voice I'd ever heard. I was practically panting just from the sound of his voice.

He got up and reached down for my hand.

"But what about the mess?" I asked.

"Screw the mess," he said as he kissed the back of my hand. He began walking backwards as he led me through the house and up to our bedroom.

"Sit down on the bed, baby." His voice was so deep my whole body trembled. He walked into the closet and after a few seconds he came back out with two boxes.

I bit down on my lower lip and said, "Do I get to pick?"

"Sure," he said with a laugh.

I looked at both boxes. One was big, like it contained maybe lingerie. The other was smaller.

I pointed to the smaller box and said, "Bigger is always better, so I want to save that one for last."

He threw his head back and laughed. "Good choice, baby." He handed the box to me and stood there with a goofy grin on his face.

I began to slowly take the wrapping paper off. I opened the box and a piece of paper was folded up in the box. I glanced up at Brad, who had a smile from ear to ear. I set the box down on the bed next to me and began opening up the piece of paper. It was a real-estate listing. *Fifty-five acres in Fredericksburg.* I glanced up and looked at Brad, confused.

"What is this for?" I asked.

"Well, I know how much you love being close to our friends, I know how much you love Fredericksburg, and now with my new promotion…" he said with an evil grin.

Oh. My. God. Is he saying what I think he is saying?

"Brad…are you saying…"

He grabbed my shoulders and pulled me into a standing position. "Yes baby, I'm saying what you think I'm saying. I want to have your dream home built on this piece of land. I want to raise our children there and I want to be closer to our friends. They've been through thick and thin with us and I don't want to be so far away from them."

I felt the tears building in my eyes. "Do they know? I mean, does everyone know?"

He let out a small chuckle. "Just Josh and Heather. They've been keeping an eye open for us. I do know that they have been talking about moving to Mason, but I don't think I could go that country! I mean, Fredericksburg has everything, but with that small-town charm."

I threw myself into his arms and began crying. "Yes! Oh my God, yes!" I pulled back and laughed. "And we can build a house? Our own house how we want it?"

He nodded. "Yes, pumpkin. However you want it."

"When? When can we buy the land?"

He looked away for a brief second before turning back to me. "I um, well, I kind of already bought it. I hope you're not mad."

I shook my head and wiped away my tears. "No…God no, Brad. I'm not mad at all. I want to scream I'm so happy! When can we start planning? I want to design the house ourselves!"

He reached down and picked up the other box. "How about we start planning after you open your next present?"

I grinned and took the box from him as I sat down again and began opening it. I took the lid off and moved the pink tissue paper out of the way and revealed a beautiful red silk and lace gown. I took it out of the box and held it up.

"Oh, Brad. It's beautiful," I whispered.

"Go put it on," he said in a low voice. I snapped my head up to him and jumped up as I quickly made my way into the bathroom. I'd never stripped out of clothes so fast in my life. I ran over to my dresser in the closet and pulled out a pair of red lace panties and then grinned. I put the panties back in the drawer and slipped the gown over my head. I stood and looked at myself for a brief second. I pulled my unruly red curls up and let a few fall down around me face. One quick spray of perfume and I was ready.

I slowly opened the door to the bathroom to see Brad lying in bed. When I stepped out he sat up. *Did he just make a growling sound?*

"My God, Manda. You look...you're...you are breathtakingly beautiful."

I smiled as I placed my hand on my stomach. I felt the butterflies dancing in there and I had no idea why. Brad got out of bed and my hungry eyes devoured his naked body. I bit down on my lip and had the incredible urge to drop to my knees and take him in my mouth. I slowly licked my lips as he moved closer to me.

"Amanda..." he whispered as he leaned over and brought his lips up to mine. The way he moved his lips against mine—teasing me with the kiss I so desperately wanted—was driving me insane.

"I want to lose myself in you, Manda," he whispered against my lips as he moved his hands along the silk gown. It felt like he was poking me with a thousand little needles as his hands traveled along my body. He began gathering up the material and smiled.

"I hate that you only got to wear this for a few minutes, but I need to be inside you, baby."

I dropped my head back and whispered, "yes," as his lips moved along my neck. When he lifted up my gown and noticed I didn't have any panties on, he dropped to his knees. He lifted my leg and put it over his shoulder.

"Brad...oh God!" I said, and I felt his tongue teasing my clit. I pushed my hips into him...I needed this more than I thought. I wanted to beg him but ran my hands through his hair. With each tug of his hair he moaned and I about fell apart.

Then I felt it building. I grabbed onto my breasts and let out a gasp. *Shit!* They were so sore it was unreal. I slowly began playing with my nipple through the delicate fabric. Then it hit me as he moved his tongue in just the right rhythm.

"Brad! Yes! Ah...oh God...yes..." I felt like I was having one of the most intense orgasms of my life. I felt my one leg wobble as I tried to remain standing up. Before I knew what was happening I was on the bed and he was on top of me. The silk gown was still on and he was teasing me with his tip. I shook my head to clear my thoughts...it felt like my body was still trying to come down from my orgasm.

"Manda, I'm going to make love to you," he whispered. He lifted the dress and I barely moved so he could lift it over my head.

"Yes, Brad…please. I need to feel you."

With that, he entered my body in one swift move. I let out a scream and grabbed onto his ass as he began to move in and out of me. The way he was moving his hips and kissing on my neck was more than I could take.

"Brad…oh God! I think I'm going to…yes…oh God, don't stop what you're doing."

"Manda…baby, come for me, 'cause I can't hold off much longer. You feel fucking amazing."

Shit! Him telling me to come pushed me over the edge. I began calling out his name over and over as he began going faster.

"Harder, Brad! Shit, go faster!" I called out.

The next thing I knew he was biting down on my shoulder as he fell apart.

Oh. My. God.

He steadied his breathing and moved his lips up to my ear and said, "You're the most beautiful woman I've ever laid eyes on, Manda. I love making love to you more than anything. I love you so much."

I felt the tears building in my eyes as he moved his forehead up to mine and looked into my eyes.

"I love that you say that to me. It makes me feel so special."

He smiled as he kissed me lightly on the lips.

"I love you, Brad."

"I love you too. Thank you so much for loving me. For believing in me."

I pulled him to me and began kissing him with as much passion as I could. I needed him to know how much I loved him and how much I did believe in him. How much I believed in our love and in our future.

He rolled off of me and pulled me to him as we both quickly drifted off to sleep.

That night I dreamed of country houses, horses, two little girls running around and Brad making love to me under the stars.

8 Brad

I woke up to someone giggling. I sat up and looked around. Amanda must have already gotten up. I stumbled out of bed and looked around for my sweats. I was exhausted. Amanda had woken me up in the middle of the night by crawling on top of me. I couldn't believe how she rocked my world again last night. I'd never had an orgasm that felt like it started in my fucking toes. I laughed as I shook my head thinking back to Jeff telling me I was in for a ride because pregnant women were horny as fuck.

My smile faded as I thought about Amanda being all alone all those months while she was pregnant with Meg. I shook my head to clear my thoughts.

As I opened the bedroom door, I heard my angel talking.

"Oh, Heather. I've never in my life felt so incredible sexy as I do now. I mean, the gown he bought me was so beautiful and elegant, but also sexy as hell. Oh, then last night—it was beyond amazing. I don't know if it was because of how sexy I felt, how happy I was about the land or just the idea of being with him that had me so insane with lust."

I leaned against the wall and listened to her going on and on to Heather. My heart was pounding a mile a minute knowing that I made her feel that sexy and that loved. It did things to my heart and even more things to my stomach. I pulled out my phone and looked at the time.

"I don't know! He just told me last night but I'm so ready to start right now! I'd love to have the house done before the baby is born. Yes! Oh God…the idea of making love to him in every room… on every surface. Fuck…I think I need to go crawl into bed with him again!"

I held in my laugh as I pushed off the wall and made my way into the kitchen. As I walked into the living room I saw Maegan playing with one of her new Christmas toys. She was in a trance and I couldn't help but laugh. Amanda jumped up and said, "Hey…my prince is up, so I'll talk to you later. Hey Heather? I'm so happy that you enjoyed your evening last night as much as I enjoyed mine," she said as she winked at me.

I smiled as I made my way over to Maegan. She smiled when she saw me and held out her hands. I picked her up and carried her into the kitchen with me.

"Good morning, my princess. Look at how beautiful you are this morning. You take my breath away baby girl. Have you had your breakfast?"

"She has. But I bet she would love to sit and eat some more," Amanda said with a laugh.

I reached in and took out a container of Hawaiian Delight baby food and began giving it to Meg. The smile on her face caused me to let out a chuckle.

I glanced over and saw Amanda watching me. I winked and the expression on her face changed. She bit down on her lip and began rubbing her one leg up and down her other leg.

"Manda?"

"Yeah?"

I let out a laugh. "Baby, are you horny?"

"Oh my God, yes! Brad, I don't know what's wrong with me but seeing you sitting there with her and...oh God." I watched as she moved her hand down into her sweatpants and began feeling on herself.

"I just want...I just want to feel you inside of me."

I jumped up and picked up Meg and made my way into the living room. I set her in her playpen and wound up some sing-along toy.

I walked back into the kitchen and walked over to Amanda.

"No...Brad, I need to see the baby."

I picked her up and brought her over to the island and set her down. We had a clear shot of Meg in her playpen. I pulled Amanda's sweats down and then her panties.

"Wrap your legs around me, Amanda." She quickly did. "Brad, the baby. We can't do this in front of the baby."

I glanced back over to Meg who was now laying down fighting to keep her eyes open. I took a few steps back and pushed Amanda up against the wall. I reached my hand down and touched her. *Motherfucker she was soaking wet.*

In one quick swift move I pushed into her. She let her head rest against the wall as she let out a gasp. "You feel like heaven. Pure heaven."

"Brad, go fast...I need you to go fast...and hard. I want it...I want you to..." she said, breathing heavy.

"Say it, Amanda," I said.

She closed her eyes and then opened them and looked into my eyes. "I want you to fuck me."

Best. Christmas. Ever.

As much as I wanted to make love to her I knew how much she just wanted to be fucked and that is exactly what I did.

"Brad," Amanda called out. "Yes...yes!"

I couldn't hold off any longer. "Amanda…ah hell baby. I'm gonna come."

"Ah…Feels. So. Good." As we both came together we captured our moans with passionate kisses. I swore I'd never had such hot sex in my life.

She looked at me and said, "Oh my God! Meg!" I quickly looked over my shoulder to see our princess sound asleep snuggled up on top of her giant Tigger.

"She's sound asleep, baby," I said as I winked at her.

"Brad," she whispered. "That was probably one of the hottest fucking moments of my life."

I threw my head back and laughed. "Yes. Yes it was, baby."

She let out a giggle and said, "I feel so naughty. I can't believe we did that with Meg right here."

"I'm pretty sure she's not going to remember," I said as I watched her putting her panties and sweats back on.

"You feel better?" I asked.

She spun around and gave me a look that about dropped me to my knees.

"Oh yes. Thank you so much. I wouldn't mind um…doing that again sometime."

I couldn't believe it but I actually felt my dick jump. "Trust me…we will be doing that again and very soon."

As we sat in Rick Thunder's office, the builder Gunner had recommended and said was the best in the area, I kept glancing at Amanda. Gunner had drawn up some rough plans of the house we were wanting. I couldn't believe how fast he had them drawn up and the suggestions Jeff had blew me away. Those two could be designing some pretty damn awesome homes if they wanted to. No wonder the fuckers had the most unique barns that I'd ever seen.

Amanda's smile never once left her face. Her parents were keeping Meg for the evening while we stayed in Fredericksburg to spend time on the property and get some alone time.

After the builder went over a few things with us, we all headed out to our property. As we walked around I thought Amanda was going to skip the whole time. She was beyond thrilled. We walked up over a hill and she let out a gasp.

"Holy hell. Look at that view." She spun around and looked at me and then ran into my arms and jumped up as she wrapped her legs around me and began kissing the hell out of me.

"Oh baby, it's perfect." After another round of kisses she whispered into my ear, "I'm having naughty thoughts about a blanket, some sparkling water and a present Ari gave me."

My heart dropped into my stomach and I just looked at her.

"Um…"

"I think we might have just found our building site," Rick said with a chuckle.

I slowly put Amanda down as she winked at me and turned around. "This is perfect, Rick. I mean, don't you think it's just breathtaking?"

He nodded and said, "I do. And it faces north and south, but if we angle the house a little you will get amazing sunsets up here."

I stood there trying to figure out what the gift was that Ari had given Amanda while the two of them continued to talk about north, south, east, west and sunsets.

After a few seconds I shook my head to clear my thoughts as I walked up to Rick and slapped him on the back.

"So, do we all agree this is the spot?" I asked as Amanda started jumping up and down.

"If it were my land, this is where I would build. It's flat, close to that barn and the view is beyond amazing." Rick said with a grin.

The property came with a thirty-by-ninety barn that wasn't too far from the location we were at.

I took a deep breath and let it out as I looked at Rick and said, "Let's do it then."

Rick held his hand out to me and as we shook, Amanda began talking about all the ideas she had. We walked back to the truck and by the time we got there it was decided by Rick that Amanda was going to be required to take five-minute breaks between her ideas.

Amanda got in my truck and I walked Rick over to his truck.

"It's a gem, Brad. You did a great job and I'm not even going to ask how you got it at the price you did."

I let out a small chuckle. "Good negotiator, I guess. So you'll get back with us, what, after the new year?"

"I'm thinking if all works out with the numbers, we can start building within the next thirty days."

I reached out to shake his hand again. "That's what I want to hear. I'd like to have my girls in the house before the new baby."

After another minute of talking, we said our good-byes, and I watched as Rick drove off. I turned back and saw Amanda leaning against the truck. I busted out laughing when I saw the blanket in her arms.

"Where in the hell did that come from?" I asked as I made my way over to her.

"Well, I knew we were coming out here and I thought it would be only fitting if we broke in the new place," she said with a wink. Then she held out a box. "A belated Christmas present," she said with an evil grin.

I smiled as I took the box from her hand. I quickly tore the wrapping off and opened it.

"Holy shit," I said as I stared at a vibrator. I felt my legs slightly give out. I quickly looked up to see her biting down on her index finger. "Motherfucker. The next eight months are going to be pure heaven," I said as I pulled her to me and kissed her. She let out a soft long moan as she moved her hand down and grabbed me.

"I want you, Brad," she whispered.

I quickly turned and looked around. *Soft, flat spot is what we need.* There was a giant live oak that caught my eye. I practically pulled Amanda's arm out of her socket trying to get her over to it.

She laid the blanket out and then pulled her long sleeve t-shirt off as I began unbuttoning her jeans.

"Son of a bitch, Manda. You make me crazy, you know that?" I said as I began kissing her neck. I reached my hand into her panties and began feeling on her. I slowly slipped two fingers in as she let out a moan.

"God…you're so wet."

"Brad…please…"

I stepped back and quickly started taking off my clothes as I watched her shimmy out of her panties and unclasp her bra. Before I knew it, she was lying down and she took the vibrator out of the box. *Oh God…is she going to use it on herself?*

I watched as she placed the vibrator at her entrance and began to slowly work it in and out.

Can't. Breathe.

I dropped to my knees and put one of her nipples into my mouth as she began moving the vibrator in and out faster.

"Brad, take yourself in your hand," she said. I snapped my head back at her. "I want to watch you."

"Motherfucker," I whispered as I lay down next to her and did as she asked. I couldn't pull my eyes away from her working the vibrator in and out. It wasn't going to take me long before I came, especially when I saw her playing with one of her nipples.

"Christ, Amanda."

"Yes! Oh, Brad."

"Faster, baby, go faster," I said.

She began moving it in and out faster and I prayed to God she would come soon because I was about to.

"Shit!" she called out, and then started moaning in pleasure.

"Oh…ah…Amanda, I'm going to come, baby," I said, and kept watching her work the vibrator.

"Brad…it looks so damn hot watching you…oh God…"

She must have been hit with another orgasm right when I began coming. I looked into her eyes as she called out my name over and over again. I leaned over and began kissing her.

She finally pulled away, trying to catch her breath. "Wow," she whispered.

"Wow is right. Damn, Manda, that was the hottest damn thing I've ever seen…or done."

She giggled and looked away. "Ari talked me into it!"

"I'm going to have to thank her when I see her New Year's Eve!"

She looked down at my exhausted dick. "Let's head back to the hotel. Give him time to recoup. I'll be wanting you again I'm sure."

I jumped up, threw on my clothes and helped Amanda up. I picked up the blanket and folded it while Amanda put the vibrator back into the box.

It was silent in the truck on the way to the hotel. "A penny for your thoughts."

She shook her head and said, "I'm just thankful that we found each other. I knew the moment I saw you that I wanted to be yours forever."

I quickly looked at her and then looked forward. I pulled into the hotel and parked the truck. I turned my body and faced her. She gave me the sweetest damn smile.

"You amaze me, do you know that?" I said, and I placed my hand on the side of her face.

"Yes. Yes, I do know this," she said with a wink. She jumped out of the truck, grabbed the blanket and box out of the backseat that held the vibrator and said, "Come on. I'm ready to get my naughty on again."

I shook my head and laughed as I watched her skipping into the lobby of the hotel.

"Shit, I love that girl."

9 Amanda

I walked up and kissed Meg on the top of her head and said, "Be a good girl for daddy." When I looked up into Brad's eyes, all I saw was fear.

"I don't think this is a good idea. What if…"

I put my finger up to his lips and smiled. "Baby, I promise. Everything is going to be all right. I'll be fine. Please don't worry, okay?"

He nodded his head and closed his eyes. "It's just… Amanda, if she ever hurts you again… I just can't move past all the things she did."

"Brad. I know you love your mother."

"I love you, more than anything," he whispered.

I felt the tears building in my eyes and my heart dropped in my stomach. "I love you more than anything, too. Just let me do this and see what happens. It's like something clicked in her when she saw Maegan. I saw it in her eyes. Let me just give her a chance. I promise if she crosses the line once I'll walk away."

He sucked in a breath of air and slowly let it out. "Fine. But one wrong thing and I mean it, Amanda."

I took my index finger and gestured across my heart. I grabbed my purse and gave Brad a quick kiss good-bye before he pulled me back to him and kissed me so deeply and passionately.

"That's to keep you thinking about me," he said against my lips.

"Hmm…I will for sure be thinking about you," I said with a wink.

As I made my way out to my car, I said a quick prayer that this wasn't a set-up by Brad's mom. When she called me last night and asked if we could meet for dinner because she wanted to talk to me and give me the baby pictures, I was reluctant to do it, but something inside me screamed that I needed to do this for Brad. I just prayed for Brad's sake she didn't ruin this.

I walked into the South Congress Café and looked around. I saw Carol sitting at a table near a corner window. *Ugh. No easy escape.* When she looked up and saw me, the smile that spread across her face surprised me. I gave a weak smile in return and headed over her way.

She stood up and gave me a kiss on the cheek and said, "Amanda, sweetheart, thank you for meeting me for dinner."

Sweetheart? I've never been called anything but Amanda.

I sat down and decided to just cut to the chase. "Carol, I'm doing this for Brad. I'm doing it because I love him more than life itself and I know not having his parents in his life is hurting him. The last thing I want to do is hurt him."

She sat back and smiled as she shook her head. *Here it comes.*

"Do you know the first time Brad brought you home, I couldn't believe it? I was looking at a mini me."

Huh? Well okay, I wasn't expecting that. I'm sure the look on my face must have been one of shock, because Carol laughed.

"I know what you're thinking. A mini you? Hell no. But you were, or rather, you are. I could see the spit and fire in your personality and see the passion for life in your eyes. I knew Brad must have really taken to you for him to bring you home. He never brought girls home."

I wanted nothing more than to say, *Gee…wonder why?*

She reached for her wine and took a sip. She seemed to want what she just said to sink in. "I'm not going to lie to you, Amanda. I hated you the moment I saw you."

And here we go…

"But I also fell madly in love with you."

"Huh?" I said out loud, not meaning to.

She let out a chuckle and continued on. "Yep. I could see the love between you and Brad and each time I saw the two of you together, I saw it grow. I think a part of me was insanely jealous. Brad was my only child. He was my baby boy. No one was ever going to take him away from me. I decided early on that I was going to make it miserable for you. I wanted you to end up leaving."

She slowly shook her head and gave me a sad smile. "But you were stronger than that. Your love for my son, I should say, was stronger. I didn't realize at the time when I was trying to drive you away, that I was driving Brad away…from everyone."

I sucked in a breath of air.

She closed her eyes for a good thirty seconds before she opened them again. "When I saw you standing there holding Maegan, and she was the spitting image of Brad, something just clicked. All the pain that I caused both you and Brad came flooding all at once. I thought I could just pretend it was you who was the problem, but in the end I needed to realize that it was me who had been the problem."

She stopped and waited. I wasn't sure what she expected me to say. *Yeah, Carol you were the problem…can I have the baby pictures?*

"I'm not really sure what to say right now, Carol," I said as my voice cracked.

She sat up just a little straighter as the waitress walked up and asked what I would like to drink.

"Water, please," I said.

She asked if we were ready to order. Carol asked her for a few more minutes.

"I just wanted to get this all out, and if you decide to leave after, I completely understand."

I slowly nodded my head.

She took a deep breath and quickly let it out. "I don't expect you and Brad to just open up your hearts and let me in. I know I have to earn that back and I'm very prepared to do so. I'd like more than anything to get to really know you, Amanda. I'd like more than anything to have my son back in my life again and get to know my grandchildren."

My heart started beating a mile a minute.

"I'd like to ask you for your forgiveness. I know I don't deserve it and I know I've never done anything to make you want me in your life, but I'd love to try and get there."

I looked around and prayed that the waitress would get there with my water. My mouth was so dry and I needed a drink before I could talk.

Right on cue she walked up and handed me the water. I took a long drink and set it down before looking back up at Carol.

I gave her a smile and said, "Well…you can start by showing me Brad's baby pictures."

The smile that spread across her face caused me to let out a small laugh. When she leaned over and picked up a giant shoebox, I really started laughing.

"I went through all the albums and pulled them out. I wasn't sure if you do that whole scanning thing or what but I sure had fun going through these."

We both let out a laugh as the waitress walked back over. I let Carol order while I quickly looked at the menu.

The waitress looked at me next. "Oh um…I'll have the mesquite-grilled pork chops.

"Good choice," she said with a smile.

As the next hour passed by, we ate, talked about Maegan, talked about Brad as a baby, looked at baby pictures, and bonded like we never had before. I sent Brad a text, letting him know things were going good.

As we left the restaurant, Carol reached for me and gave me a hug.

"Thank you, Amanda. Thank you so much. I've had a lovely evening."

I smiled and thought back to when I used to work for her. We actually had a few occasions where we got along so good and even laughed a lot.

"I'm really glad we did this, Carol. I think this will be great for Maegan to be able to know both her grandparents. But mostly, I think this will really help Brad to continue to heal and move on. He still holds onto a lot of pain and guilt. But with the baby, and now y'all coming back into his life...I think things will be even better for him."

She grinned and nodded her head. "I certainly hope so."

She gave me a kiss on the cheek, and we made plans for her and Brad's father to come out for dinner after the new year.

Driving home I was overcome with the incredible sense that everything was as it should be. Things happen for a reason and I truly believed that for Brad to be completely free of his past addictions and fears he needed this more than any of us.

I couldn't wait until New Year's Eve. It was going to be a new year, new beginnings, new relationships, and a new sense of believing that my husband was the happiest he's been in a long time.

10 Brad

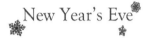

New Year's Eve

"You are officially getting your man card revoked," Jeff said to Josh.

"Fuck you, asshole," Josh said as he got up and grabbed another beer from the cooler and sat back down. "No one is revoking my man card."

"Dude, you watched *The Notebook,* alone," Jeff said with a serious look.

Gunner started laughing and shook his head. "That is a good movie, I have to say."

Josh jumped up and pointed at Gunner. "See! Gunner watched it. Why can he watch it and it's okay, but if I watch it, I'm a pussy and get my man card revoked."

I looked over at Scott's best friend from college, Lark, who was sitting there, just taking it all in with a smile.

Jeff took in a deep breath of air and blew it out. "Gunner can watch it 'cause he's Gunner. He's a romantic pussy who lost his man card years ago."

Gunner sat up and said, "Hey!"

Lark lost it laughing, as did I. Jeff continued on with his explanation as to why Josh must lose his card.

"You, on the other hand, are not Gunner. As much as you'd like to think you're romantic, you will never be like the master himself," Jeff said, and pointed toward Gunner, who stood up and took a bow.

I shook my head and took a sip of water as Josh stood up to plead his case.

"Uh, excuse me, asswipe, but I kicked your asses with my song to Heather, let's not forget that. I kick your asses every day, you just don't know about it. I got up and went out the other morning and found wildflowers, in December mind you, and made a little bouquet and brought them up to Heather with breakfast and fresh squeezed orange juice. Then I gave her a certificate to go and get a message while I watched the kids for the afternoon. When she got home I had one of her favorite meals cooked, had the kids washed, fed and ready for bed. Don't tell me I'm not romantic."

He looked around at each of us. No one said anything for a few seconds until Lark said, "Holy fucking shit. You're whipped, dude." Lark threw his head back and laughed some more. We all laughed and Josh just sat there, shaking his head.

"Okay, I will say that was pretty good, Josh." Gunner said.

"Thank you, Gunner. I'll just say Heather appreciated it and I was rewarded very nicely that evening."

"You're still getting your man card revoked. I'm logging on when I get home," Jeff said as he pulled out his phone. "If I thought I could get a signal, I'd log on now and do it."

Josh looked at him and shook his head. "Dude, are you kidding me? If you do that I'll revoke your card."

"For what?"

Josh tilted his head and looked at Jeff. "*Twilight?*" Josh said as he winked at Jeff.

Jeff sat up and dropped his mouth open. "How do you know about that, you little fucker?"

Gunner, Lark and I all leaned forward. *Oh, this was gonna be good.*

"What about *Twilight?*" Gunner and Lark said at the same time.

Josh gave Jeff a smirk and said, "Jeff here, who claims not to be pussy-whipped, watched all the *Twilight* movies with Ari. Might I add…all the movies one right after the other. *Twilight* marathon."

Gunner leaned back and let out a chuckle. "Damn Josh, you're reaching now."

"Oh, I'm not done," Josh said. "Not only did Jeff watch the movies with Ari, he invested hours into reading the books."

All of us busted out laughing as Jeff rolled his eyes. "Fuck you, Josh. You read *Fifty Shades of Pink.*"

Josh shook his head, "It's *Fifty Shades of Grey,* you stupid shit, and you had Ari read it to you!"

"Hey, that was a good book. I let Amanda read it to me, too, and my dick had never been so exhausted in my life as it was when she was reading that book to me," I said with a smile and wink over towards Josh.

"Shit dude, tell me. Ells wanted to try almost everything in the book. That book should be like some kind of required reading for men," Gunner said with a laugh.

"Dude! Jesus H. Christ. That's my sister. I don't need to hear that shit. I think I might have just thrown up a little in my mouth," Jeff said as he punched Gunner in the arm.

"Oh hey, you know what are good books? It's that one series where the guys eat a lot...damn, what's it called again?" Josh said as he tried to remember the name of the books.

"Oh hell, Amanda and I read those, their last names are Bradford, right?" I said with a chuckle.

"Yes!" Gunner and Josh both said at the same time.

Lark stood up and looked around at all of us. "Holy hell. All of y'all's man cards are officially revoked for twenty four hours."

We all looked around. "Wait. Dude, are you serious?" Jeff asked with a panicked looked on his face.

"Hell yeah I am. You're all a bunch of pussy-whipped, chick-flick watching, and romance-reading girls. Give them up. Now."

"Son of a bitch. Good going, Josh!" Jeff said as he reached for his wallet and took out his man card and gave it to Lark.

"Gunner? Fork it over." Gunner cursed under his breath as he took his card out of his wallet. "You don't know what it's like though, Lark. I mean, if you just gave it a try you'd like watching..."

Lark held up his hand and stopped Gunner from talking. "No. I'm pretty sure I'd rather jack off in a field of prickly pears then watch a chick flick. Guaranteed sex or not, no fucking way."

Josh and I handed Lark our cards as he put them in his wallet. "Thank God Scott's talking to Garrett, because if I ever find out he has watched a chick flick...oh I don't even want to think about it."

"He has," we all said at once and then laughed.

Lark's mouth dropped open. "This is exactly why I like being single." He began pointing to all of us. "This reason right here. Pansy asses." He turned and walked toward the large bonfire of Christmas trees, mumbling something about chick flicks, books and pussy-ass men.

Jeff looked around at each of us and then down to the ground before looking back up. "Damn...I feel lost without my man card. Just knowing it was there in my wallet and now...damn."

I glanced up and saw Amanda talking to Heather. She was smiling about something and just seeing how happy she was caused me to smile. I was shocked when she had come home from dinner with my mother with a box full of baby pictures of me, and a smile on her face. When I asked her how it went she replied back with. "Great!" and then told me all about her dinner with my mother.

She must have sensed me watching her because she looked over and winked at me. I winked back and gave her the best panty-melting smile I could muster. She smiled bigger and then said something to Heather. Heather nodded her head and Amanda started walking toward me. She walked right up to me and then sat down in my lap.

"Hey baby," she purred into my ear as I moved my hand up her sweatshirt.

"Hey back at ya," I said as I kissed her gently on the lips.

Amanda looked around and said, "Jesus, did a puppy die or something? What in the hell is wrong with all y'all?"

"Got our man cards taken away by Lark," Josh said as he kicked the dirt. Heather came walking up and must have heard him, because she started laughing. She wrapped her arms around him from behind and whispered something to him, causing him to smile from ear to ear.

Ellie came skipping over and skidded to a stop. "It's almost midnight! Eeepp! Gunner, will you throw a few more trees on the fire?"

Gunner jumped up and stumbled before Ellie reached out to him. "How much have you had to drink?" she asked as she looked at Jeff with her hands on her hips.

"Oh my God. Why are you looking at me like that? He's a grown man, I didn't make him drink!"

Ellie gave Jeff the evil eye and then turned back to Gunner. "Baby, don't drink anymore. I need you to not be drunk so we can…well you know," she said as she winked at a smiling Gunner and then grinned at Jeff.

"Yuck. Gross. You're a brat, Ellie." Jeff jumped up and made his way over toward Ari. He walked up behind her and picked her up and spun her around before setting her down and turning her around to face him. He kissed the shit out of her as she smiled from ear to ear.

I rubbed Amanda's back and said, "Gunner, I'll help you throw a few trees on." Amanda quickly gave me a kiss and then looked at her cell phone. "Oh gosh. Just fifteen minutes!"

Gunner and I quickly threw three more Christmas trees into the bonfire. The heat coming from it was perfect for this chilly night. Everyone began making their way over to the bonfire.

We all stood around the fire as each person said one thing that was for him or her, the best part of the last year. Of course Amanda said the birth of Meg. I couldn't pick one…I had so many. When it was my turn I just smiled and said, "My wife's love." It was her love that pulled me back from the brink. It was her love that saved me from so much.

We counted down to zero and then kissed our loved ones. Before I kissed Amanda, I glanced over to all my friends. They were all kissing and laughing. I turned and looked into Amanda's eyes.

"Happy New Year, pumpkin," I said as I placed my hand on the side of her face.

"Happy New Year, Brad," she whispered to me, before reaching up on her toes and bringing her lips to mine. As we kissed, every happy memory from last year just flooded my mind.

"To a new year filled with nothing but happy memories and lots of love," Amanda said as she pulled away and looked up at me.

I grinned and nodded my head. I didn't doubt what she said was true. I was going to be able to be home with her and Meg. Be there for every step of the pregnancy and build my wife her dream home.

Yes. Yes, it was going to be a year filled with lots of happy memories and even more love.

She tilted her head and looked at me. "Do you think this year will be the best yet?"

I couldn't help but smile bigger and let out a small chuckle.

"Yeah, baby. I believe anything is possible with you by my side."

Amanda bit down on her lower lip as I leaned down and captured her lips with mine. I wasn't sure how long we kissed for, but all I knew was I had never been so happy and so at peace in my life. I thought back to how Bryan had told me in therapy I only had to believe. Believe in my own strength. Believe in the love of my friends and family and believe that only I had control of my future.

As I stood there and held my wife in my arms I thought about that word. The definition of *believe* is to "accept as true."

I smiled to myself and looked up at the night sky as I whispered, "I believe."

11 Amanda

August—The Birth

The pain. Shit, I don't remember this kind of pain before. I grabbed onto the side rails and tried to ride out the contraction. Brad was just about to tell me to breathe through it when I held up my hand.

"Stop! I swear. To God. If you tell me. One. More. Time. To breathe. Through the pain. I'm going to make you hurt."

"Ah, duly noted. No more breathing through the pain," Brad said with a smile.

"Brad, go find the damn nurse and tell her I want the epidural now!" I said through gritted teeth.

"Honey, are you sure?"

I snapped my head and looked at him.

"But the plan, baby. You told me if…"

I grabbed him by the t-shirt. "I swear to God, Brad, if you ever want to have sex with me again, you'll find that bitch and tell her I want the epidural…now!"

Brad quickly spun around and headed out the door. I took a deep breath and tried to concentrate on something other than the pain. I closed my eyes and pictured our new house. It was breathtaking. The baby's room had been painted in a beautiful pastel green that Brad picked out. Josh made all the furniture, and I cried when they gave it to us at the baby shower.

Maegan's room was painted pink with a butterfly theme. Brad said every time he walked in there he felt like someone had thrown up Pepto-Bismol all over the walls. I was so happy with how the house was coming together. We had only moved in a few weeks ago and just in time. This baby was ready whether we were or not.

Brad came walking back in with the nurse and another guy.

"Amanda, I'm the anesthesiologist that will be administering the epidural."

"Oh, thank God!" I said as I felt another one coming on.

"Jesus…hurry, will you please, doctor? I think she's pissed because I ate spicy food last night."

He laughed as he shook his head. "All right, let's do this."

As I looked down at my beautiful daughter, I couldn't help but think of how much had happened in the last year and a half. I moved my finger all along her sweet face as I listened to everyone talking. Taylor had been passed all around to everyone. Alex was already in love with Taylor.

I glanced over to Brad and gave him a wink. He lifted his eyebrows and walked over to me. He leaned down and kissed Taylor and then he kissed me oh so sweetly on the lips.

"I'm so proud of you, Manda. You amaze me." He whispered.

I let out a giggle and said, "I'm sorry for calling you a bastard."

"'Fucking bastard' I believe is what you called me."

I rolled my eyes and put my hand up behind his neck and pulled him to my lips again. As he stood back up he looked down at Taylor and shook his head.

"My God. Two girls," he whispered.

I let out a chuckle. "Yep, two girls. Two beautiful girls."

Brad turned and looked at Jeff holding Luke. "I'm telling you, that's the one to look out for…right there. Mark my words, if he's anything like his father…"

I laughed and caused Taylor to startle.

Jeff saw us looking at him and he walked over.

"Manda, she's beautiful," Jeff said as he reached down and gave me a kiss on the cheek.

"Thank you, Jeff. Brad here seems to think little Luke is going to be the player in the bunch," I said with a wink.

Jeff threw his head back and laughed. "Oh hell yeah, he will be!"

Luke said, "Hell yeah!"

"Oh! Oh no buddy! Don't say that. That's a bad, bad word," Jeff said as Brad's mouth dropped open and he slowly looked back at me.

"Oh God," Brad said as he closed his eyes. "My little girls."

I let out a laugh and shook my head. "Don't worry baby, they will always be daddy's little girls."

He slowly smiled and reached for Taylor. I handed her to him, and he began rocking her as he smiled and said, "You better believe it. Daddy's little girls forever."

Printed in Great Britain
by Amazon.co.uk, Ltd.,
Marston Gate.